WEATHER OR NOT

TRACY BROGAN

OLIVER HEBER BOOKS

PRAISE FOR TRACY BROGAN

"Brogan brings her signature wit and whimsy to this delightful trio of historical stories."

— *USA TODAY BESTSELLING AUTHOR*
ELIZABETH ESSEX

"Whether writing contemporary rom-com or light-hearted, gilded age historicals, Brogan always delivers!"

— *USA TODAY BESTSELLING AUTHOR*
ALYSSA ALEXANDER

"Brogan's voice is distinct and irresistible, offering both laugh-out-loud scenarios and moments of poignancy. Secondary characters enhance the hilarity and add a sense of community sure to tug at the heartstrings."

— *PUBLISHERS WEEKLY*

"Brogan creates a charming small town where even the scandals and secrets are relatively wholesome. Events sweep readers along, making them long for the idealized community Brogan portrays."

— *PUBLISHERS WEEKLY*

"Brogan knows how to capture her readers attention."

— *RT BOOK REVIEWS*

"Heart, humor, and characters you'll love. Tracy Brogan is the next great voice in contemporary romance."

— *NEW YORK TIMES BESTSELLING AUTHOR KRISTEN HIGGINS*

"Brogan shows a real knack for creating believable yet quirky characters, providing surprising emotional twists along the way."

— *BOOKLIST*

"With trademark humor and lovely, poignant touches, Brogan's books are charming, witty, and fun."

"Brogan successfully blends a sassy heroine and humor with deep emotional issues and a traditional romance. The well-developed characters and sweet story with just a touch of heat will please readers looking for a creative take on romance."

HIGHLAND SURRENDER features plenty of action, romance, and sex with well-drawn individuals – a strong yet young heroine and a delectable hero who don't act out of character. The story imparts a nice feeling of "you are there" with a well presented look at the turbulent life of the 16th century Scotland."

"Treachery and political intrigue provide a well-textured backdrop for a poignant romance in which a young girl, well out of her depth, struggles to reconcile what she *thinks* she knows with what her *heart* tells her. HIGHLAND SURRENDER is a classic sweep-me-away tale of romance!"

CHAPTER I

There are only a handful of legitimate reasons to be awake at four thirty in the morning, and even fewer reasons to be up, dressed, and standing outside in a torrential rainstorm. At the moment, Allison Winters was beginning to wonder if her reasons were valid enough to warrant her current level of saturation. Surely there were easier, drier, later-in-the-day ways to make a living, but everyone in her line of work had to pay their dues, so on this wet, blustery morning in May, she was paying hers.

As the weekend meteorologist for Channel 7 News in Glenville, Michigan, that often meant standing on the rooftop of the station during what most logical people would refer to as *the middle of the night*. And more often than not, it meant getting up close and personal with moody midwestern weather. Most days she didn't mind the unpredictable outdoors, and when inside the station, she enjoyed the comradery shared among her colleagues during those quiet hours when the night owls and the early birds collided.

But lately the zero-dark-thirty shifts had started taking a toll. She was tired of eating her lunch at the crack of dawn. Tired of having to skip nights out with friends because she was either working a double shift and covering the evening weather, or because her bedtime came at an hour when most toddlers were still up and ready to party. And she was tired of being the littlest fish in a modest-sized pond. Her two-year contract was up soon, and she was considering a change. Or at the very least, she was considering the possibility of considering a change.

"Cue Allison. In five, four, three, two…"

She swiped rain from her face as instructions from Frank, the segment coordinator (who was nice and dry inside the control room), sounded through her earpiece. She nodded at the cameraman, some new kid whose name escaped her, and swiped again before the shot went live. Not that the swipe did any good. It was too windy to hold an umbrella and she'd stood under water-falls that produced less moisture than the rain clouds above her head, but so be it. There were people out there who'd be getting up soon for work, and she owed it to her audience, miniscule though it may be at the present hour, to let them know what to expect from the skies today.

"It's a big, sloppy, wet one out today, folks!" she said, plastering on a quasi-cheerful smile. "Get out those umbrellas and raincoats because this extreme precipitation is expected to continue on throughout the day." She delivered the rest of the forecast trying hard not to blink against the pelting droplets, then tossed the segment back to the weekend anchor (who was also warm and dry inside the studio—not that she was bitter).

"Annnnd, Allison, you're clear," Frank announced through the earpiece. "When you get inside, Jessica wants to see you right away."

Allison took one step then halted, the foul weather suddenly second on her mind. "Jessica? As in Jessica Jackson, our news director?"

"Yup."

"Why is she at the station? It's not even five a.m. And it's a Sunday."

But Frank was gone, on to announcing camera shifts to the floor directors and setting up the next segments. The camera kid was already heading inside through a narrow door that led to the stairs. He paused, looking at her expectantly. "You coming? Or are you waiting for the ark?"

She smiled distractedly and followed him in, her shoes squeaking on the linoleum steps as she made her way downstairs and toward the dressing room. If Jessica was there, it had to be important. Allison shivered from a chill that had nothing to do with the rain dripping down the back of her neck, and hoped it was a good kind of important and not a bad kind of important.

In the four months since Jessica Jackson had joined the station as news director, Allison had interacted with her only during the staff meetings. Partly because their work obligations rarely had them crossing paths, and partly because Jessica intimidated the heck out of her. She was stoic and intense in a way that Allison could only hope to emulate, and her focus was always on substance and professionalism. While Allison worked hard to be taken seriously as a scientist and a meteorologist, she had an unshakable fear that Jessica found her frivolous. And she'd never get bumped to a better shift if the news director didn't think she'd earned it.

Allison eyed herself in the mirror of the tiny dressing room, trying to decide if she should change her clothes or freshen her makeup but decided that, at the moment, speed was more important than style. She hung up her raincoat, and simply wrapped a towel around her head before heading down another flight of stairs toward the executive offices.

In spite of the predawn hour, Jessica looked as polished as always, in a close-fitting pantsuit the shade of pink peonies. A surprising choice, perhaps, but she was the type of woman who could wear any shade outfit and still command the room as if she were wearing a military uniform. Her hair was pulled back in a no-nonsense bun high on the crown of her head. Allison instantly regretted the towel and pulled it off as she tapped lightly against the frame of the open door and hoped against hope that her blond hair wasn't sticking up in every direction. She could have at least pulled it back into a ponytail, but it was too late now.

"Good morning, Jessica. Frank said you wanted to see me?" She couldn't keep the question out of her tone. The one that said *Um, do you really?*

Jessica waved her into the room. "Yes, Allison. Come in. Shut the door, please. There's something I want to discuss with you."

Shut the door? Uh oh, that couldn't be good.

"Is it good news or bad news?" she blurted out, as if the ten-second warning would give her time to prepare, but Jessica's onyx-eyed gaze was enigmatic.

"Most news is neither good nor bad. It's just news. As in this case."

Spoken like a seasoned news director. *Just the facts, ma'am.*

"Sit down." Jessica motioned to the chair.

She stepped forward and her wet shoes made such an unfortunate farty noise that Allison nearly felt the need to say, "excuse me," but certainly Jessica knew it was her shoes,

right? Honestly, why was she so nervous? She settled gingerly into the chair, feeling like a seventh grader being called to the principal's office for chewing gum in algebra class.

Without preamble, Jessica said, "I'd like to send you on assignment with a storm-chasing team. You'd leave on Tuesday for Kansas and be gone for a week."

"A storm-chasing team?"

"Yes." She let that linger out there and Allison couldn't help but note that, for a newsperson, Jessica was being very stingy with the details. After a pause, the news director rested her folded arms on the uncluttered desk and continued. "You'll be expected to tape two to four segments per day. Your reports need to be entertaining as well as educational and informative. If the weather is suitably interesting, we may have you do some live reporting. Do you think you can do that?"

"I'm sure I can," she answered brightly. In truth, Allison had no idea if she could, in fact, do that, but she was a jump first, figure it out later kind of person, and she'd be damned if she didn't give this her best shot. Especially since this was exactly the break she'd been waiting for. Segments from the road? With a team of storm chasers? Viewers loved storm chasers. Her street cred would jump by leaps and bounds, not to mention that this was a surefire way to reach a broader audience, and hopefully impress her boss. "May I say I'm honored you have the confidence in my work to send me on this assignment."

Jessica took a calm sip of coffee from her Channel 7 mug. "My assessment of your abilities remains to be seen but the chief meteorologist seems to think you can handle it. It's a week on the road in a cramped vehicle with adrenaline chasers who are probably more interested in footage than science, and the chance of you seeing any truly remarkable weather is questionable. Hannah Freemont will be your videographer. You'll share a room. Still interested?"

"Yes, absolutely." She didn't know Hannah other than to say hello while passing in the hallways at the station, but she guessed they were around the same age, twenty-eight, and had the same work ethic. Surely Hannah would be equally motivated to make this trip worthwhile. They'd be fine.

"All right then." Jessica picked up a manila folder

from her desk. "Here's the rest of the information you'll need, and, Allison, I'm sure it goes without saying that I expect focused, high-quality reports that the station can be proud of. We're one spot behind Channel 4 in the Nielsen ratings and it's no secret I was brought on board to surpass them. They just got a traffic helicopter, and if we want to compete with that, we'll have to pull out all the stops. I need you to go find us a tornado."

Allison nodded, accepting the folder. "I promise you'll get the very best from me, Jessica. I won't disappoint you."

"I'm glad to hear that."

Sensing this meeting was over, Allison rose from the chair and walked out of the news director's office and around the corner before doing a silent jig of joy in the hall. Finally, an assignment with some sparkle to it, and a chance to really show Jessica what she was capable of. Catching sight of the oversized clock on the wall, she realized she had just enough time to try to fix her hair before heading back up to the roof for her next segment. Then there were the radio spots to phone in, graphics to make, and a dozen other things to handle before her workday ended. The folder and its information would have to wait, so it wasn't until she'd gotten home, changed into comfy sweats, and microwaved some soup for dinner before she opened it. Two pages in, the spoon clattered against the side of the bowl and chicken broth splashed onto her sleeve as she read the names of who she was about to spend seven days—and evenings—with.

No, no, no.

Just… anybody else.

She could storm chase with anybody. Except Dylan Parks.

CHAPTER 2

"Ride-alongs? Seriously? Who the hell approved ride-alongs?" Dylan Parks' scowl was only half serious as he stuffed a couple of clean but wrinkled tee shirts into the well-traveled duffel bag sitting on his bed.

"I did. We need the cash." Chris, his storm-chasing partner and the best driver Dylan had ever worked with, picked up a sock that had fallen to the floor and tossed it at his head.

Dylan caught it and added it to the bag, even though the mate was still somewhere on the floor. Then he nodded. "Cash is handy, but you know how these tagalongs always slow us down. They like to stop and stretch their legs. They want food and bathroom breaks, and if they aren't getting in the way of the shot, then they end up talking too much on the video. There's a huge weather system developing south of Woodward, Oklahoma, and it looks to be a crazy day. We need to get our crew on the road in the next hour."

Chris handed him the leather toiletry bag sitting on the wooden dresser. "Not a problem. All the guys are already here, and our guests should arrive in the next fifteen minutes or so. It's a meteorologist and her shooter so at least they'll know better than to talk over any video."

Dylan looked up from trying to wrangle the toiletry bag in between the tee shirts. He knew *shooter* meant videographer, but it was the other word that caught his attention.

"Her? One of them is a woman?"

Chris grinned. "Even better. They're both women."

Dylan shook his head slowly. "Did you not hear what I just said about bathroom breaks?"

Truthfully, he had no issue with women meteorologists, or women videographers, or women in general. His mother and his sisters had kicked his ass more than once, and he knew better than to suggest that a woman wasn't as capable as a man. Except at one thing. Peeing into a Gatorade bottle when there wasn't time to stop the car. The storms developing in the south were going to be vast, and would move fast, and his team had to keep up with them. They'd missed two opportunities last week to get any decent footage thanks to a broken tailpipe that needed repair, and this week was all about catching up.

"She knows the drill, Dylan," Chris said. "I talked to her on the phone yesterday and she sounds cool. Plus, it's good money for nothing more than having them ride in the back seat and do a few segments from the road."

"Road segments? You don't think those will slow us down?"

Chris arched a dark eyebrow. "That's ironic coming from the guy who takes forty-five minutes every day to style his hair. Before going out into a tornado."

Dylan laughed with acceptance and bent to pick up the other sock. "Yeah, yeah, yeah. Okay. We'll make it work. Hey, could you check the batteries for all the cameras? I meant to do that last night."

"Already done. I also restocked the first aid kit, filled up the water bottles, loaded the cooler, put Rain-X on both the Blaster and the Sidewinder, dropped your dog off at the neighbor's house, packed up the drone, and did about ten other things to get us ready. Unlike you, I don't need ten hours of beauty sleep. I've been working since seven this morning so, you're welcome. Now get your shit together so we can get out of here." He turned and strode away, whistling the *Jeopardy!* theme song.

"I'll be ready in ten minutes," Dylan called after him.

"Make it five."

They both knew it would be fifteen.

Chris was the business side of their team, deftly handling all of the day-to-day stuff. Dylan, on the other hand, was the visionary and the risk-taker. They were both meteorologists, but while Chris was all about details and gadgetry, Dylan had earned a reputation for having an uncanny instinct about which storms would turn into tornadic supercells, and which of those supercells would ultimately produce funnels. It was a good balance between the two of them and over the past three years of working together, they'd ironed out any kinks in their system. Except that Chris was always early, and he was always late.

Dylan finished packing and headed outside to the driveway of the house he and Chris rented. The rest of the crew were milling around, tackling various chores. Shaggy-haired Rob, their own videographer, was loading camera equipment into the Sidewinder, an SUV that served as their backup vehicle. Tech wizard Beau was fiddling with wires from the back seat of the Blaster, their primary vehicle, and twenty-two-year-old Nathan, their other driver and an aspiring forecaster, was sitting in a dinged-up lawn chair staring intently at the laptop perched on his long, spindly legs. His ever-present Cubs baseball hat was turned with the brim at the back of his head, adding to his youthful appearance.

Off to the side of the driveway, standing in the grass with their backs to him, were Chris and two women, obviously their guests for the week. The shorter one had deep-red hair woven into two braids. Her khaki shorts were topped with a shapeless blue tee shirt, and she held a small video camera close to her shoulder. Then Dylan's gaze traveled to the woman next to her—and stuck. She was a pony-tailed blonde in a dark-purple tank top and black yoga pants that clung tightly in all the right places. She was tall, slender, and had, quite frankly, the best ass he'd seen in a long time. He blinked and adjusted his sunglasses. If the front side of her was half as good as the backside, he'd have to remind his guys—and himself—that ride-along guests were off-limits. Not that he wouldn't welcome a little female companionship, but this was a workday. And he was a professional.

"Up there we have a Vantage Vue portable weather

station," Chris said, pointing to the roof of the Blaster. "It's pretty reliable, and, you know… portable. In addition to our own staff, we work with Channel 17 quite often and they have a Doppler on Wheels mounted in the back of an F-150. Then, just to keep all our bases covered, I always have my Kestrel 3000."

"Kestrel 3000? That sounds like a Quidditch broom," said the redhead.

Chris chuckled and pulled one from his pocket. "It's this thing. A handheld weather station. It tracks wind speeds, temperature, wind chill, heat index, dew point." He handed it to her, and she gave it a two-second glance before handing it back. "What about those pod things that you leave in the path of tornadoes? Do you guys have one of those?"

"Sometimes. We don't have any to deploy this week, though. We do have a drone but so far haven't had much luck launching one. If you get on the right side of the funnel, the drone will get sucked into the vortex, which is what you want, but more often than not the wind shear just smashes it back down to the ground."

Dylan listened to the exchange as he made his way toward them, his footsteps crunching over the gravel driveway. The blonde turned at the sound, and he blinked again, removing his sunglasses, certain that his eyes were playing a not-very-funny trick on him.

Because if he didn't know better, he'd say that woman in the distracting yoga pants next to his partner was Allie Winters. But it couldn't be. It definitely couldn't be, because the last time he'd seen her, she'd been returning his engagement ring and twisting his heart up like an F5 tornado.

CHAPTER 3

"Hi, Dylan. Um, surprise?" Allison tried to smile but the muscles in her cheeks decided to twitch instead of relax so all she could offer her ex-fiancé was a slightly sheepish curve of her lips. Even that was an effort. So was breathing. If hyperventilating into a paper bag was an option, she would have considered it.

She'd had a few days to prepare for this moment but seeing Dylan in person was still enough to render her both light-headed and heavyhearted. He looked good. Very good, with sharper angles to his face and more bulk to his shoulders. His dark hair was cut much shorter than he used to wear it, while his eyes were the same bright blue that had lingered in her memories for years. She'd seen photos of him here and there on social media because they had a few of the same old friends, but she'd avoided those as much as she could. She hadn't wanted to know what he was up to. Not because he hadn't been important to her, but because he had.

Dylan halted in place, color suffusing his face, and she recognized how lame her greeting was. She should've warned him, or told Chris to warn him, but truthfully, she was afraid if Dylan knew she was coming, he'd find some way to avoid her. And after the initial shock of seeing his name on that paperwork, she'd realized that *she* very much wanted to see *him*.

"Allie?" His voice rasped, and he quickly coughed to disguise the rattle. "Wow. I… wow." To his credit, he closed the distance and gave her a hug. Sort of. It was the kind of hug you might give an aging relative with fragile bones who always smelled of Chapstick and arthritis cream. The kind that *looked* like a hug but that involved virtually no bodily contact. He took a full step back a millisecond later and she could all but feel the cold front moving in.

"I didn't know you were our ride-along this week," he said, his voice neutral, expressing neither dismay nor joy. Her heart and stomach did a turbulent little cha-cha.

"I didn't know you'd become a storm chaser," she answered. She stole a glance at Chris, wondering if he knew any of the history between her and Dylan, but his mirrored sunglasses betrayed nothing.

"Wait, you guys know each other?" Hannah asked, lifting the camera to film the answer.

Allison nodded, wishing she'd filled her shooter in on the details. They'd had plenty of time to kill during the flight from Michigan to Kansas, but she hadn't wanted to make it a *thing*. So instead, she and Hannah had talked about families and movies and laughed over the fact that they'd both, at some point during their preteen years, kissed a poster of Justin Timberlake. Hannah had admitted to being in a friends-with-benefits situation that was nearing its expiration date, but when she'd asked Allison about her relationship status, she'd simply said, "I'm not dating anyone right now."

That was true. She wasn't. And she hadn't. Not really. She'd had the random two- or three-month sprees with a few guys over the past couple of years, but work was her number one priority, and none of those dates had inspired her to focus on anything different. None of them had ever compared to Dylan either, but that was a fact she'd tried hard to ignore.

"We worked together in Sandusky," Dylan answered, putting his sunglasses back on and turning toward the truck. "I see Chris is giving you ladies the four-one-one on all the electronics. He's the guy for that, so I'll leave you to it. We'll head out soon."

Allison watched him walk away and tried not to think about the last time she'd seen him do that, a tsunami of hot, sticky remorse cascading over her. Guilt over their breakup was like a tattoo she couldn't just scrub away. Although she'd tried.

Chris finished showing them around and introducing them to the other guys, and soon they were on the road, with Allison and Hannah in the back seat, sitting behind Chris and Dylan. Allison wished she could switch sides with her videographer, so she didn't have to stare at Dylan's profile all day, although he seemed to have adjusted to the surprise and was taking the high-pressure situation in stride. Not that he had much choice. As the miles passed, the conversation flowed easily enough, but with all topics restricted to weather and storm chasing.

"We communicate with our guys and other teams by cell phone most of the time, but sometimes there's no service out here in the plains, especially when the wind kicks up, so we also keep a set of walkie-talkies charged and ready. Some chasers have ham radios, but we don't bother with that." Dylan was giving them a basic tutorial of what equipment was found inside the truck, and it was plentiful. All the while he kept a laptop open with radar showing the storm system they were trying to catch up to. "We have a police scanner, a weather radio, and some old-school maps, again, in case we lose Wi-Fi. Not that the paper maps do us much good. We stay on paved roads as often as we can, but it seems like more often than not we're flying eighty miles per hour down an unnamed dirt road and hoping we don't get stuck in the mud."

"Why don't you have one of those tank things? Those cars that look like a giant metal beetle," Hannah asked. Her questions so far had been basic, but Allison was glad since it kept the conversation going without much effort from her.

Dylan chuckled. "I assume you mean an intercept vehicle, like on TV? We don't have one because they're as expensive as hell and hard to build. Underneath all that armor is a truck chassis but by the time they're finished, those things weigh about eight tons and get maybe ten miles to the gallon. We like being a little more nimble, but that does mean we can't get as close. It's a trade-off."

Dylan continued on, talking about weather patterns and what they watched for. He explained to Hannah about wall clouds and rotation and hooks on the radar. Most of it was information Allison already knew but listening to his excitement made her smile. It was one of the many things they'd had in common, a geeky love of the weather, and his words triggered a flash flood of memories. Afternoons spent watching cloud formations float by, of challenging each other with forecast speculations, of evenings spent laughing and teasing and encouraging each other. He'd been her biggest fan once. But that was a long time ago, before prevailing winds had sent their lives in two different directions.

DYLAN WAS RAMBLING on like a first-year meteorology student, but he couldn't seem to help it. He had about fifty intense and conflicting emotions creating a blizzard in his brain right now, leaving little room for logical thought and no idea which way to turn. He was a mess and struggling hard not to show it. What the hell was Allie Winters doing in his back seat? And how was it possible she was even more beautiful than he'd remembered? She was like a sexier, more serious version of her past self and that was not good news. Sure, he still had a stash of printed pictures of her somewhere, stuck in a drawer or a shoebox, and even one picture in a frame. A photo of the two of them nestled up on a sofa, with her wearing one of his Ohio State sweatshirts and him looking smug and satisfied because they'd just had sex with each other for the very first time. He knew it was stupid to keep that picture, but he could still remember how he'd felt in that moment. He'd felt like a man with nothing but blue skies ahead. It was the moment he knew he'd marry her someday.

Only he hadn't.

He'd proposed to her, about a year after that photo had been taken, and she'd said yes. That was the best moment of his life. Then two weeks later, she changed her mind. He'd never felt so gutted, not before or since. Looking back, she may have been right about them being too young. Twenty-three seemed like a lifetime ago, but he wished she'd given them a chance. Given *him* a chance. She'd put her career first without even a discussion. It never had made sense, but he'd worked hard to make peace with it. He'd moved on, even getting close to proposing to another woman last year, but something had held him back and he'd ended the relationship instead. Now, with Allie sitting just a few feet behind him, he couldn't help but wonder if she'd been the ghost haunting all his other relationships. Because in the mix of all the emotions battling inside his skull right now, several of them had to do with him still wanting her.

The storms picked up and he tried to focus on that, but none of the impressive clouds he'd had his eye on turned tornadic. That wasn't atypical. There were roughly thirteen hundred funnel clouds per year in the United States, but storm chasers were lucky if they caught more than a few dozen, and more often than not, those funnel clouds came in clusters because storm systems needed all the right elements to come in to play. The science of forecasting improved with each passing season but, just like having your ex-fiancée show up in your driveway, tornadoes were unpredictable.

They stopped by the side of a creek and Allie, donning a black blazer over her tank top, did some short, taped interviews with the rest of the crew. Chris and Beau talked about the tech they relied on while Nathan nervously stared at the ground and mumbled something about why he wanted to be a meteorologist. When Dylan's turn came, Allie gazed right into his eyes and his adrenaline kicked in as if no time had passed between them. His heart had far too good a memory, but he shut that down as best as he could to focus on her interview.

"What made you decide to be a storm chaser?" she asked, holding a microphone up to his mouth. He took a breath to calm his pulse. If the question had come from Allie, his old girlfriend, he might have said, "I was restless and bored because the life I'd wanted with you had evaporated." But the question was from Allison the TV meteorologist, so he gave the sales pitch answer instead. "Meteorology and storm-chasing technology has come a long way, but we still don't know why some supercells form tornadoes when others don't. We don't know why some funnel clouds last for a few minutes and others might last for an hour or more. So, the more scientific data we can gather, the more we learn about wind speeds inside the funnel, both horizontal and vertical, and the better we'll be able to predict violent weather. And the more lead time we can provide, the better equipped we'll be to keep people safe."

She stared at him for a second longer and he wondered if he was supposed to say something else, but then she thanked him, turned to the shooter, and signed off on the segment.

"Thanks," she said to him again after Hannah walked away and it was just the two of them next to the stream.

"For what?"

"Um, for being a good sport today. I'm sorry about surprising you."

"Well, you've surprised me before. This one was a lot easier to handle." His tone was sharper than he intended, yet all things considered, that was about the nicest way he could put it. But her smile dimmed, eclipsed by the harshness of his words and he instantly regretted them. But why? Why did he feel bad? *He* shouldn't feel bad. He didn't dump her. *She* dumped *him*. With no warning. Still... there wasn't much point in holding on to that anger. It was a lifetime ago, and he was *over* it. He was over *her*.

Right?

Damn it. This was going to be a long week.

CHAPTER 4

"So, maybe it's none of my business but are you going to tell me the scoop between you and Loverboy? Because the sexual tension in the car today was suffocating." Hannah sat cross-legged on the rust-and-green plaid bedspread of a budget motel, eating cheese crackers as Allison pulled a floral nightgown from her bag.

All she wanted to do was take a long, hot shower, put on that nightgown, and go to bed. Amazing how exhausting it could be sitting in the back of an SUV all day, but she knew her fatigue wasn't really from that. Dylan had been cordial, even after the interview, but when he'd made the comment about being surprised by her, it was a sucker punch in the gut, a terrible feeling that she just wanted to get rid of. And every damn time he called her Allie, it took her right back to the time when *they* had been an *us*.

She sank down onto the bed next to Hannah.

"We were engaged." The words came out on a long, sad sigh.

Hannah dropped a cracker, and her mouth went nearly as round as her eyes. "Engaged? I figured there was some hanky-panky or something but engaged? That's huge. What happened?"

Allison hated stirring up the long-buried feelings, but it was unavoidable now. "We were around twenty-three and both doing internships at the same little station in Sandusky. We lived together for a while. Then he got offered a job in Sarasota."

"Oh! And then he dumped you? Just like a man." Hannah stuffed a half dozen crackers into her mouth and started chomping furiously.

"No, he didn't dump me." Allison shook her head, her chin dropping with the weight of her memories pulling it down. "He proposed, and I was going to go with him. But then I got offered a job in Chicago, and I just couldn't turn it down." She paused again, the words reluctant on her tongue. "Dylan was basically the perfect boyfriend and I loved him so much, but I also worked really hard to get through school. My parents sacrificed so much to help pay for it, and I know if I'd gone with him, my career would've taken a back seat."

"Couldn't he have gone with you to Chicago? There must have been other job opportunities there."

Allie had often wondered about that herself, along with a myriad of other what-if type questions. What if she had married him? What if he'd called her after their breakup? What if she'd called him? What if? What if? What if? But none of that mattered now because it was in the past. "I didn't ask him to. And after I broke things off, he just moved away, and we haven't spoken since. Not until this morning."

Hannah handed her a conciliatory cheese cracker. A little square of processed comfort carbs. "Well, a little heads up would've been nice," she said. "I only got a bit of your reunion on tape, and it could've been good stuff."

"I don't think that's what Jessica is looking for. In fact, if she'd known there was any history between me and Dylan, she probably wouldn't have let me come, and I need these segments to be amazing. I'm trying to get promoted."

A soft *harrumph* came from Hannah. "Okay, well, just so you know, the stuff we have so far is pretty meh. Hopefully we'll get some better shots this week, though.

Chris said the storms on tap for tomorrow should be more intense."

Allison was quickly learning that Hannah was not one to sugarcoat things. "Was I meh, or was it just the circumstances? Because I need to not be meh."

Hannah shrugged and handed her a few more crackers. "You seemed a little tense but given the circumstances, I guess I see why."

A gentle knock rattled their motel room door, and Rob's voice permeated through the wood. "Hey, you guys want some pizza? We're hanging out in our room."

The women exchanged glances.

"These crackers are not doing it for me," Hannah said, rising and pulling Allison up from the bed. "Let's go have pizza. Unless you'd rather just hang out here?"

That was a tough call. A hot shower and a few hours relaxing in a quiet room versus what was sure to be greasy pizza in a tacky hotel room with Dylan and all his crew. The key word being Dylan. Would he even want her there? Her stomach growled, making the decision for her. Dylan would just have to deal.

Two slices, two beers, and two hours later, Allison was feeling full and significantly more relaxed. The crew's friendly banter now included her and Hannah, a pleasant perk to the evening indicating they'd been accepted. Dylan continued to be sociable but professional, which was probably for the best. He'd showered and changed into jeans and a white tee shirt, and as the alcohol mellowed her edgy nerves and lowered her emotional defenses, she momentarily felt an overwhelming urge to press her face against his neck just to see if he still smelled as good as she'd remembered. Realizing where her mind was headed, she switched to drinking water and strategically moved to a chair farther away from him. She needed to focus on doing a kick-ass job this week, and not get distracted by Dylan's good smell.

"Allison, where did you go to school? What's your background?" The question came from Rob, who'd been sitting next to Hannah most of the evening under the guise of discussing photography, but Allison suspected other motives. He was cute in a coltish, sloppy way, and Hannah didn't seem to mind his close proximity. That friend with benefits might be losing his place.

Allison leaned forward from her spot on a lumpy motel room chair. "I got my bachelor's in atmospheric science from Michigan State. I did an internship up in Marquette, and then I spent some time in Sandusky."

She'd leave it vague, just as Dylan had. "After that, I took a job in Chicago."

"But aren't you back in Michigan now?" Rob asked.

Dylan was across the room, leaning against a beige laminate dresser and talking to Chris, but she sensed he was tuned in to what she was saying. Especially once she'd mentioned Chicago, the catalyst of their breakup. "I am back in Michigan, yes. Chicago wasn't a great fit for me. It's pretty cutthroat in that size market, and then my mom started having some health problems so when a job in Glenville came up, I took it. I do the weekend weather. It's a pretty good place to be."

"You said an internship in Marquette?" Nathan interjected. "That's way up there, isn't it? Like practically Canada?"

"Practically. But separated by Lake Superior. It's gorgeous there in the summer but brutal in the winter. Way too much snow for me. Reporting during blizzards is my least favorite thing, when you can't see anything and the cold keeps draining your earpiece batteries."

A couple heads around the room nodded in agreement. With various levels of forecasting and broadcasting experience among them, they started comparing disastrous reporting stories, and times when weather had gotten the best of them. Stories of storm-chasing mishaps were revealed, some clearly embellished and oft-repeated, like a game of telephone with each person adding their own spin. Allison found herself laughing right along with them, and more than once, caught Dylan's gaze resting on her, like a snowflake landing on her skin. It was strange to be in the same room, as if none of the sadness had ever happened. As if they were back in Sandusky and sharing one of those sweet nights that ended with whispers and kisses under the covers. That part had always been good for them. All of it had been good for them, except their timing.

"I've got to get to bed," announced Hannah shortly before midnight, putting an end to the impromptu tacky motel greasy-pizza party. They'd be getting on the road early the next day, probably heading back toward Kansas City if the weather systems they were tracking stayed on their current path. Dylan kept his distance as the women said good night to everyone, but then came outside right behind Allison.

"Hey," he said softly, prompting her to turn around. Hannah kept walking. "I'm sorry to hear that about your mom and the health stuff. What happened?"

It was dark, but the yellow lights of the motel gave everything an amber hue, and the sounds of distant traffic could just barely be heard over the wind rustling the tree branches.

"Congestive heart failure," she answered. "Turns out smoking is bad for you."

"I'm sorry," he said again. She thought he might step forward and hug her, properly this time, but he stayed put, just outside his motel room door.

"She's better now. Making lots of lifestyle changes and managing pretty well. Thanks for asking."

"Sure. I always liked your mom."

"She liked you too."

They stared for another moment, and she wanted to say more, but then Nathan came outside, breaking the fragile spell.

"Oh, sorry," he said, eyeing them both before ducking his head and darting toward his own room.

Dylan chuckled; his smile small but sincere. He offered up a short sigh. "Good night, Allie."

"Good night, Dylan."

CHAPTER 5

"So, are you going to tell me what happened between you and the hot weather babe?" Chris asked, not bothering to stifle his yawn. He was still in bed the next morning, although Dylan was uncharacteristically up, dressed, and ready to go, pouring water into a tiny coffee pot sitting on the counter next to an ice bucket. He didn't respond to the question.

"Well?" Chris prompted, tossing off the covers.

Dylan shrugged. "Not much to tell. We dated for a while. And then we didn't." *She broke my heart and left me for dead. But I'm over it.*

"Uh-huh. Is that why you turned Buckeye red the minute you saw her? And why you've shaved for the first time in two weeks? I haven't seen your face so baby-ass smooth in I don't know how long."

"Shut up," he said without heat, taking the joke in stride. Chris would understand but Dylan just didn't want to talk about it. "She was… important. But it was years ago. I'm over it." Saying it out loud didn't make it feel any more real. He *was* over her, but having her around stirred up a lot of memories and a lot of emotions that he'd much rather leave unexamined.

Chris wandered into the bathroom, flipping on the light and standing there in a gray tee shirt and plaid boxers. "Are you sure? Maybe her being here isn't a coincidence. Maybe she tracked you down to see if the old flame was still burning."

Dylan shoved the coffee pot back into its spot. He *really* didn't want to talk about it. "Damn, Chris. I had no idea you were such a helpless romantic."

"I believe the phrase is *hopeless* romantic."

"Yeah. I know." Dylan grinned, determined to change the topic. "Now get your shit together so we can get on the road."

Half an hour later they were outside in the motel parking lot, and the weather was perfect, if perfect meant ideal conditions for supercell formations. It was hot, humid, and he could practically feel the instability in the atmosphere.

Chris ambled up next to him and sniffed the air. "Smells like tornadoes. Let's get going."

Nathan rushed forward and set his laptop on the hood of the Sidewinder. "Check out this system," he said giddily. "The radar is blowing up."

Dylan peered at it for a scant second and agreed. Yep, today would make up for all that driving around yesterday, and he was ready. More than ready. He wondered if his eagerness to see some impressive weather was amplified by his desire to encounter a funnel cloud or two for Allie. It's what she was here for, after all. Maybe he wanted to impress her a little bit too. Prove to her that he was good at what he did. Because he was, and if that impressed her? He was okay with that. Because wanting to *impress* her had nothing to do with *wanting* her in general. Right?

She and Hannah emerged from their room a few minutes later, travel coffee mugs in hand. He noted that today's stretchy exercise pants had the same emotional effect on him as yesterday's had, which was damned inconvenient. In all honesty, hearing her laughter last night hadn't done him any favors either. Neither had catching a whiff of her perfume as she'd passed by or watching her press a bottle of beer to her lips as she drank. Being around her was messing with him far more than it should. Yes, she was still beautiful, and yes, he was still attracted to her, but he'd taken this ride once before and it ended with an ejector seat straight into misery. No thanks. He'd be polite, and even considerate. He'd help her get her job done, and maybe they could even have some fun doing it because he was a make-the-best-of-it kind of guy, but if she was here chasing anything other than weather, she was too late.

"Let's get this show on the road," he said, opening the car door for her as she reached his side. She smiled up at him, and he reluctantly found himself smiling back.

"How's it looking today?" she asked innocently.

He deliberately glanced at her cleavage. Because, hey, *cleavage.* "It's looking pretty good from here," and he heard her chuckle as she slid into the back seat.

"THIS IS the system we're following," Dylan said, pointing to the radar screen of his computer as the Blaster traveled north on Interstate 183. "Based on these forecast models, I'd put money on supercells developing near Hays, Kansas, by midafternoon. This system is moving at about forty miles per hour, and we should be ahead of it soon. That's right where we want to be."

Allison nodded, anticipation rising inside her like a helium balloon. Her tornado forecasting skills were woefully untested, but she agreed with his assessment. Looking out the window she spotted low clouds on the horizon that appeared to be full of moisture and perfect for producing a storm. And hopefully perfect for getting some great footage. This morning in the motel room, she and Hannah had reviewed her segments from yesterday and they weren't awful, but they weren't awesome either. Just average, but average wouldn't impress her news director. And average wouldn't get her promoted to a better time slot.

As it had yesterday, conversation inside the car revolved mostly around weather-related topics such as forecasting technologies and industry politics, but it also took a few verbal detours toward more pressing matters, like which Avenger had the most impressive skills, whether or not craft beer was worth the upcharge, and if rap musicians were the twenty-first-century version of troubadours. That was Hannah's theory, prompting laughter by all as both the men said in unison, "What the fuck is a troubadour?"

When they stopped for gas, Dylan casually followed Allison into the adjacent convenience store and down the candy aisle. They perused for a few seconds before she spotted what she wanted and grabbed two red-and-yellow bags.

He scoffed good-naturedly. "Honest to God, Als,

you're the only person I've met in my entire life who actually eats Raisinets."

She smiled. "Well, somebody else must be eating them or they wouldn't keep making them. Maybe you just need to broaden your scope. You know, meet more people?"

"I meet plenty of people. I just happen to know that you're *unique*."

Her laughter caught in her throat. He'd said it to tease her, of course, but his cheeks flushed immediately, his knowledge of her candy preferences a spontaneous and accidental reminder of their shared past. She felt her own cheeks heating up, and suddenly she wanted to ask him each and every question that had lingered since their breakup. Was there anyone else? Had he been in love again? Did he miss her or hate her or worse yet, had he stopped thinking of her at all? She could hardly expect otherwise. She'd left him. He didn't owe her any of his brain space, but the intimacy of his innocent comment stirred up far more questions than either of them could answer while standing in the lackluster candy section of a dingy roadside convenience store with fluorescent bulbs buzzing above their heads and twangy country music playing in the background.

But later… she'd ask him later. At some point before this week ended, they would need to talk. Really talk.

For now, she simply plucked a Snickers from the shelf and held it out to him. "Still your favorite?"

He eyed it for a moment, as though she were holding a baited mousetrap rather than candy, but then his lips slid into an easy smile. His eyes met with hers, and his fingertips oh-so-casually grazed over her hand as he took the Snickers, sending stupidly delicious tingles zinging every which way inside of her.

"Still my favorite," he said, holding her gaze, and making all those zinging tingles suddenly zero in on the most logical, yet least convenient, spot of her whole body.

While her brain may have had other plans, and her heart had worked hard to get over him, she still had one lonely erogenous zone that had never really forgotten him. Other lovers had been clumsy or rushed or too much of this and not enough of that, but Dylan had been just right. He *knew* her, her rhythms and her needs and her vulnerabilities. He'd known when to be playful and when to be earnest. And he'd trusted her to know all the same things about him, but she'd tossed that all away for a career. A career that often left her standing on the rooftop in the rain. And *always* left her with no one to go home to.

CHAPTER 6

"See that rain wall?" Dylan's voice rose with excitement as he pointed out the open window of the Blaster. "Chris, how far away do you think that is?"

Chris leaned forward from his spot in the driver's seat to get a better look off to the west. "I'd guess about a quarter of a mile."

Dylan nodded, leaning his head and shoulders out of the car for a second before popping back in. "Let's pull over for a minute." He turned toward the back seat. "Allie, this looks like a good place to do a segment. We've definitely got some strengthening rotation overhead. Looks like a funnel may be trying to tighten and drop."

"We can get closer," Chris said, but Dylan shook his head.

"No, this is close enough for now. Another couple of minutes and we may have to get back in the car."

Chris stole a glance in Dylan's direction but pulled over to the side of the two-lane road and rolled to a stop. On either side of them, fields stretched out as far as Allison could see. There was a single farmhouse in the distance, a faded red barn next to it, and a smattering of trees here and there while above them hovered darkening, ominous clouds pulsing with energy.

"That is one scary looking sky," Hannah said as they clamored from the car.

"You are not wrong," Allison agreed. As a meteorologist, she'd seen her share of powerful weather, but it was more of the thunderstorm and blizzard variety. This was something else entirely. This system was big and real and roiling right above their heads. Her hands trembled as she scrambled to clip on her microphone pack.

"Dude, why are we so far away?" called out Nathan as he, Rob, and Beau scrambled from the Sidewinder behind them lugging various forms of recording equipment.

"We're giving Allie a chance to do a segment before this supercell unleashes," Dylan called back. "Get whatever footage you can."

She felt a rush of gratitude at Dylan's answer. His

job was to get his crew as close to the action as possible but even after everything she'd put him through, he was willing to have his entire team stop here just for her benefit. It was a sacrifice and incredibly thoughtful. Now she owed it to each of them, as well as to herself and Jessica Jackson back at Channel 7, to do a skillful job of reporting. She certainly wouldn't have to fake the adrenaline coursing through her system. She was excited and nervous and scared and thrilled. And a little nauseous at the thought of that system overhead getting even meaner, as if Mother Nature were on a hormonal rampage.

"Can I get you on camera for this?" she asked Dylan as he walked toward the edge of road, eyes on the sky. "Could you describe what you're seeing for the viewers?"

He turned back to her, his fast smile a bright flash under the darkening sky. "Sure. Come stand over here and with any luck we'll capture a funnel dropping during your report. I'll just keep talking until it does!" His enthusiasm was infectious, and she smiled back, setting aside her concern that he might actually be right. Judging from the looks of that sky, a tornado could unleash at any moment to reach down and pluck them from the ground. It was like wanting to see a ghost but not *really* wanting to see a ghost because that would just be too flippin' scary. She wanted to see a tornado, but when faced with the reality, *did she*?

Ignoring her fear, she and Hannah quickly ran over a few details as she threw on her TV meteorologist blazer. She couldn't very well report in just a tank top, and within seconds, the videographer had the camera poised and ready. Dylan stood next to Allison with the fields behind them and the undulating storm system overhead, a wonderful and exciting backdrop.

"This is Allison Winters with the Channel 7 Weather Team. We're fortunate today to have meteorologist and storm-chasing expert Dylan Parks as our guide. As you can see, we've got some severe weather developing. Dylan, can you tell me what's happening in the atmosphere right now?"

"Absolutely, Allison." He turned to the camera like a pro, far more relaxed today than he had been yesterday. "Folks, we've got a robust supercell forming just east of Ridgemont, Kansas, and all signs point to this system being a prolific tornado producer. Right now, we're about four hundred yards from a rapidly rotating rain wall and I can see by the cloud formations that there's a significant rotational updraft. What most people may not realize is that it's not only the circular motion of a funnel cloud that does damage. It's also the vertical winds inside the tornado. It's those suction vortices, sometimes multiple vortices inside one tornado, which cause the most destruction. So far, we don't have a way to measure that vertical wind speed, but we know it's even more intense than the outer bands of the storm."

Allison nodded, and rather than adding her own observations, she prompted him with another question because he was a natural in front of the camera. He'd been fine at reporting back in their Sandusky days, but this new and improved Dylan was polished and sure of himself. His easy charm lit up as he talked about wind speeds and air pressure and stovepipes versus wedges. His style was thoroughly engaging and in the back of her mind, Allie was thinking it was a shame he wasn't on-air all the time. Then again, she might not be the most objective viewer at the moment because, standing so close to him, she was thinking as much about his face as she was his words, but still, he was mesmerizing.

A few more questions and weather-related banter left her pleased and optimistic. The segment was fun but professional, engaging and informative. Thanks to Dylan, Allison was going to deliver just what her news director wanted. She wrapped up just as drizzle started to mist the air.

"How was that?" he asked, his smile turning a little sheepish.

"Amazing. You're really good at this. I sincerely owe

you one."

"There's an understatement." His voice was low, and a subtly crooked eyebrow indicated he was teasing, but her response was cut short, becoming a distressed yelp as a bolt of lightning arced across the sky. The sound cracked, reverberating in the air around them and she instinctively grabbed ahold of Dylan's arm.

Hannah squeaked loudly at the same time. "Damn, that's bright on camera!"

"Back in the trucks, everybody." Chris called out the instructions, but his guidance was entirely unnecessary since they were all already scrambling like circus clowns trying to jump into a too-small car. Nervous scuffling and laughter turned to relief as soon as they were back inside the relative safety of the vehicles, slightly damp from the rain and thoroughly energized by the potentially near-death lightning strike.

"That was a little too close," Chris said, putting the SUV in gear and pulling back onto the road. "I think it singed my nose hair."

"I'll be sure to include that detail in my report to Channel 17," Dylan replied as he put the phone to his ear to call the station. "Hi, this is Dylan Parks in the Blaster. We've got rapid upward motion just west of Dumont. I'm looking at my screen and that hook is coming around pretty fast. Do you see it on the radar?"

The rain increased as he continued talking, and Chris drove them toward what any logical person would be heading away from. Something plunked against the roof. Hannah ducked, clearly not enjoying any part of this. Allison looked over to see her shooter's cheeks pale in the bluish light of the storm. Another plunk sounded, followed by another.

"I think we've got hail," Allison said, and sure enough, the plunking grew more rapid and loud. She peered out the window to see marble-sized hail bouncing on the ground.

"Shouldn't we be slowing down?" Hannah asked, struggling to keep her camera poised in her shaking hands. "It seems like we should be slowing down."

But Chris didn't slow down.

"We're in good shape, Hannah," he answered. "This one is traveling away from us." As he spoke, more lightning flashed.

"There it is," Dylan exclaimed. "A cone coming down. You see it?" He was talking to them while also delivering information over the phone, his voice getting louder as his words tumbled out. Allison tried to make out the formation. They passed a tiny cluster of trees next to the road and suddenly, there it was. A fully formed funnel reaching from the sky. It appeared to be moving in slow motion, a graceful, gentle thing, but of course, it wasn't. She knew that and her heart jumped into her throat. She could hear Hannah all but hyperventilating in the seat next to her but could not take her eyes off the storm.

The tornado grew, stretching from the clouds until it made contact with the grassy field, and Allison was glad to see that, for now at least, there appeared to be nothing in its path other than farmland. It was an oddly morbid sort of excitement—being so thrilled to watch something so destructive—but the power of it had to be honored. Dylan continued talking to the TV station, Chris kept driving, and Hannah kept the camera pressed to her window capturing as much as she could. Meanwhile, Allison had the luxury of simply watching and observing, hoping to soak in every part of this so she could retell it on air.

They followed the funnel for what seemed like forever, and yet no time at all. They were at the mercy of the sky, and she was so fully captivated, it was hard to determine just how long they'd gone on. But then the rain decreased, and just as suddenly as the funnel had appeared, it magically withdrew. She glanced at her phone to see it had been less than fifteen minutes, but an experience that would last her a lifetime.

A minute later the rain stopped completely, and both Chris and Nathan pulled over to the side of the road so the crew could catch their collective breaths. While everyone else jumped from the car, thrilled with the chase, Hannah emerged much more slowly, her complexion now decidedly green.

"You going to toss some cookies?" Beau asked her. "It's okay. You wouldn't be the first one."

Hannah's expression went from pathetic to grateful, then she bent at the waist and puked into the tall, wet grass on the side of the road. Allison started to move toward her, but lanky Rob got there first.

"She's okay," he called out, giving the group a thumbs-up with one hand while he patted Hannah's back with the other.

"How about you. Are you okay?" Dylan asked, suddenly next to Allison.

Okay?

Was she okay?

She was better than okay. She was ecstatic!

She beamed up at him, flooded with exhilaration. "I am fantastic! I loved it!" She very nearly threw her arms around him but caught herself at the last second.

He smiled back. "That's my girl. I thought you might like it. And you didn't really get to see much that time because of the rain wall. The good news is this system isn't finished with us yet. After we regroup, I think we can find you another one."

CHAPTER 7

Dylan was on a mission. He was always on a mission when they were chasing, but this was different. Seeing Allie's excitement from that modest funnel cloud made him more determined than ever to encounter something truly impressive. Fortunately for him, nature was providing, and the supercells were producing one after another. The rain had cleared, leaving the air hot and sticky with visibility significantly improved. He spotted indistinguishable pieces of debris swirling up into the air surrounding a massive wedge they'd encountered just moments earlier.

"Let's stop for a second. I think we can jump out for some footage. You up for it, Hannah?" he asked.

"Oh, sure." Her voice betrayed her lack of enthusiasm, but Dylan had to hand it to her. She was tough. After that first bit of hurling, she was right back in action. You didn't become a news videographer if you couldn't handle seeing rough stuff, but even the toughest couldn't always handle the motion sickness triggered by hanging out in the back seat of an SUV and watching everything out your window spin in circles.

"That thing is massive," Allie said breathlessly, her eyes round with awe as she came to stand next to him. The rest of the crew gathered around the Blaster with each of them holding up some kind of recording device.

"And loud," she added.

"Sounds like a jet taking off, doesn't it? I'd say it's about five hundred yards away," he all but shouted as he pointed at his phone to get some video. "And about a quarter of a mile wide. See how the whole updraft is rotating? That thing is going to cause some real damage."

"There go some power lines!" Nathan's voice crackled with nerves and excitement as flashes of light popped in the distance and dust kicked up from the earth. As they watched for a moment, the group was uncharacteristically quiet. Chris stood a bit behind the rest of them, talking to Channel 17 on his phone.

"We don't have much more time," Dylan said. "That

thing is on the move, and I don't want to end up too far away from it. Allie let's just get some video of you with the funnel in the background and you can just add a voice-over later. It's too loud for good sound quality anyway."

He started to step away so she could be alone in the shot, but she reached out a hand to stop him, her face betraying no small amount of concern.

"You want me in the video?" he asked.

She nodded again, and he smiled as she gave a thumbs-up to Hannah, who had stepped back to frame the shot. He could see from the light on the camera that she'd already started recording. As they faced the storm side by side, he leaned close to her ear. "You okay, Als? This one is definitely a monster."

She'd be fine, and her fear was healthy. Only a moron would be this close to such violent weather and not have a healthy dose of anxiety. Her earlier enthusiasm was now tempered with some good old-fashioned common sense.

"I'm good. I just can't believe how gigantic it is. The clouds fill the entire sky, and that funnel looks like a skyscraper. I just can't wrap my head around the scope of it." She leaned into him as they stood watching. Dylan tried not to read anything into it, her closeness, her pressing against him, but damn it felt good to have her there, to *feel* her, especially while sharing something that was a major part of his life. His arm went around her waist, as much from old habit as hesitantly rekindled interest. He'd been fighting the attraction since she'd shown up in his driveway and it was getting tedious. Given the circumstances, maybe it was worth exploring that a little. What was life without risk, anyway?

Far too quickly Chris, who was always the voice of reason, said, "Guys, that thing is growing and moving fast. I think we should get back on the road." His partner was right, but Dylan was reluctant to let Allie go. His arm, of its own accord, tightened around her before dropping away, and her shy smile told him she didn't mind the extra squeeze.

Back in the car, they drove on for nearly fifteen miles before the funnel finally dissipated. In spite of its size and intensity, the destruction appeared to be minimal and no one had been injured. For that, Dylan was grateful. It was the dark side of what they did, seeing the aftermath of the wind's fury, especially when people got hurt. Today, scattered power outages, a handful of damaged homes and businesses, and lots of shredded tree branches seemed to be the worst of it, so his crew's general mood was elation tempered with fatigue as they stopped for the night at a roadside motel just north of Townsend.

"Anybody hungry? I'm starving." Beau pulled a metal case full of computer equipment from the back of the Sidewinder to take inside his motel room. "There's a barbeque place across the street."

While murmurs of agreement came from the others, Allie caught Dylan's eye. She leaned toward him. "Do you think maybe we could, you know, have a little time? Just the two of us? It seems like maybe we should… talk."

God, he wished talk was a euphemism for something else. They did need to talk, of course. They had a lot to discuss, and he had a lot of questions, but after today's excitement, what he mostly wanted to do was kiss that spot just above her collarbone in the way that had always made her sigh with pleasure. Would she still? Would she melt into him the way she once did when he pulled her close? Better yet, would she wrap her legs around him if he pressed her down against a mattress? Because that's what he wanted to do. Sure, he wanted to talk, but mostly he wanted to take her to bed and remind her of all the ways they were good together.

His response was far less specific. "Sure. How about we meet back here in half an hour? I could use a shower, then we can grab something to eat."

Her response was equally neutral. "Sounds good. See you in half an hour."

"Do I need to find someplace else to sleep?" Hannah teased as she dropped off her bag in their motel room. "Because I will if you want me to. Just leave a sock on the door."

Allie couldn't stop the blush, or the chuckle that bubbled up in her throat. "No, you do not need to find a different place to sleep. Dylan and I just have a bit of... reminiscing to do. That's all."

"Are you sure? Because he's been leering at you like a man who just got released from prison. Does he know that you're just *reminiscing*?"

"Of course, he does. My gosh, Hannah. This is a business trip, for goodness' sake. Not a booty call."

Hannah pulled off her tee shirt and replaced it with a clean one. "I'm not judging, mind you. To be perfectly honest, I think you should climb all over that. I won't tell anyone. Besides, you guys were engaged once. This one wouldn't even count."

Allison laughed out loud at that. Hannah's suggestion was tempting, and she certainly couldn't say she didn't want to. Watching Dylan work today had been a thrill, but even more than that, it had been fun. It wasn't just seeing the tornadoes, it was observing him in his element. *Dylan* made it fun, and if memory served—and it did—he knew how to make rolling around in the sheets pretty damn fun too. But where would that get them? Other than the obvious perk of having had great sex, of course. But was that a good enough reason? Her emotions were already as tangled up and gnarled as some of the twisted trees they'd seen demolished by the winds, and any kind of physical interaction would only complicate things. Sure, she couldn't deny that every instinct told her to go for it, but truthfully, it was a risk even just going to dinner. There was so much history, and she'd ended things so very ungraciously. There was just no telling where the night would lead them. Crying was a distinct possibility.

"I think it would still count," she said to Hannah, "but I'll keep you posted. If I don't come back to the room, well… don't wait up."

Allison showered as quickly as she could but by the time she was out of the bathroom, Hannah had already left for dinner with the others, and she was a bit relieved. She desperately needed a few minutes of quiet before facing Dylan across a table. Over the past few days, they'd been able to chat without ever leaning in toward anything substantial, but when it was just the two of them in a restaurant, there'd be no place to hide.

She put on the one sundress she'd brought with her, stashed among the leggings and tank tops and her single on-air blazer. It wasn't dressy and she hoped it didn't seem like she was trying too hard, but this occasion did call for something at least a hint nicer than what she'd been wearing. She left her hair down, whipped on a little mascara and lip gloss, and grabbed a denim jacket in case it cooled off later. All of that had taken twenty-five minutes, so she sat down on the edge of the bed and waited. She didn't want to be the first one outside, even though it was silly to just sit there. Then she pondered the idea of maybe going straight to his room, skipping dinner altogether, and just having her way with him. He'd probably be a pretty good sport about that. Her cheeks heated up at the thought even as her intellect warned her it was a terrible idea.

Instead, she waited three more minutes, then left the room. Dylan was already outside, leaning against the Blaster and staring at his phone. He looked up at the sound of her shutting her motel room door, and his smile was slow and dangerously sexy. He liked the sundress. She could tell.

"I didn't think you'd be ready yet," she said, feeling stupidly anxious and totally at a loss for clever words.

He was wearing jeans with a blue-and-white striped polo shirt. Nothing fancy but it set her heart to skipping.

His broad shoulders gave a little shrug. "I was motivated." He moved away from the SUV and slid his phone into his back pocket. "There's a little pub-type place down on the corner. Want to go there?"

"Sure." *Again, she was so very clever…* Conversation at dinner just might be a study in monosyllabic speech.

The walk to the pub took just a few moments and soon they were seated at a square table with a multitude of initials carved into the surface. Looking around, Allison realized most of the other tables had carvings too. It seemed to be a theme. Other than that, the inside of the pub was uninspired, with cheaply paneled walls and a green velvet–topped pool table over in the back corner where a couple of scruffy men of indeterminate age and social graces were playing a round. Neon signs advertised various brands of beer and liquor, and a dartboard hung on the wall right next to the restroom sign, leaving Allison to wonder how many people walked out of the bathroom and got nailed in the forehead with a dart.

It wasn't very crowded, with only a dozen or so other diners, and at least their table was next to an oversized window, giving them a full view of the tiny town. Not that it was much to look at. It didn't matter though. She'd probably be staring at Dylan most of the evening anyway.

"Hi, folks. Do you know what you want?" A pudgy server wearing a black tee shirt that very nearly but not quite covered her belly handed them each a plastic-coated menu. "Don't get the cod. It's today's special but just trust me. I don't recommend it."

Dylan chuckled and smiled up at her. "What do you recommend?"

"I recommend you eat someplace else." She burst out laughing and thwacked her notepad against the edge of the table. Allison and Dylan laughed, too, exchanging equally bemused stares.

"No, but seriously," the server continued, sobering up as abruptly as she'd laughed. "Other than the cod, everything is surprisingly good. I like the shepherd's pie and we sell a lot of lasagna." She bent closer, displaying an impressive length of cleavage, and put a hand to her mouth as if to impart a secret. "It's Stouffer's so it's pretty good."

Allison nodded. "Good to know. Maybe we could have a minute to look over the menu?"

"Sure thing, honey. I'll be back in a minute with some water."

Dylan smiled over at Allison, his expression apologetic. "I'd suggest we look for someplace else, but this may be the nicest place in town, and at least they serve drinks."

"I'm good with it. And I haven't had Stouffer's lasagna in a long time."

CHAPTER 8

This bar was a D-list dive. Normally Dylan wouldn't have even noticed. He and the guys ate at places like this all the time because they typically had the best greasy cheeseburgers, but tonight it would've been nice to find someplace with just a bit more ambience. A bit less grime. He had no idea how the conversation with Allie would go, or what twists and turns it might take, but tonight might very well be the last time they shared a meal together, just the two of them. The last time they'd been to a restaurant, she'd dumped him. At the very least, this night had to go better than that one had.

The server returned and jotted down their order. "You folks hear about that twister south of town?" she asked. "It was all over the news. Sure as heck am glad it didn't do much damage here, although my cousin did lose part of his chicken coop. Then again, that thing was half falling down already. A butterfly could have tipped it over."

"We did hear a little something about the twister," Dylan said, handing her his menu. Typically, he would've mentioned the storm chasing but this waitress was already on the chatty side. If he told her why they were in town, she'd likely pull up a chair and yakkity-yak with them all night. He didn't want to hear more about her cousin's chicken coop because, regardless of how much trepidation he had about anything Allie might have to say, he wanted to get that conversation going. He wanted it out of the way. If it went south, he'd finish his beer and call it an early night. But, on the off chance that it went well... No, he couldn't even let his mind wander in that direction. Not yet.

"So...," Allie said, after the server delivered their drinks, a beer for him and a vodka and cranberry for her. "Um... how *are* you?"

He stared at her for a moment because, for such a simple, basic question, it had a lot of potential layers to it.

"I'm not quite sure how to even answer that," he

finally said. "I mean, I'm good. If somebody had asked me last week how I was, I would've said I'm great. I love my job. It's full of opportunities. I have a great crew of guys to chase with. In the off-season I work at the National Weather Service. My bills are paid. I have a dog. So, it's all good, for the most part, but right now I'm sitting across from a woman who dumped me after I'd proposed. I haven't spoken to her in almost five years and suddenly she shows up in my driveway, unannounced, and says she's going to spend the week in my car, watching me do my job, and you know what? That has me feeling just a little off-balance. How are *you*?"

Damn. He didn't mean to sound so sarcastic, and he hadn't intended to unload on her that way. He didn't even realize he'd been stuffing all that shit down. Maybe because he hadn't been forced to think about it in a very long time, but with her right there in front of him, it all just kind of spilled out. He saw her eyes get sparkly with moisture. He didn't want her to cry, and he certainly didn't want to be the reason for it, but... maybe she did owe him an explanation. Something more substantial than *we were too young*.

She blinked and pressed her lips together for a second but maintained his gaze.

"What kind of dog?" she asked softly.

His brain tried to register the ridiculousness of the

question and against his better judgment, he let out a chuff of laughter. "Seriously?"

"I thought we could start with the easy stuff. What kind of dog?"

He sighed but started to relax again. He could play this game if she wanted to. "A Bernese Mountain dog–lab mix. Her name is Judy. I didn't come up with that. She was a rescue."

Allie nodded and took a drink. "Cute. When you work for the weather service, do you stay in Lawrence, or do you live someplace else?"

"Chris and I rent that place in Lawrence, and we have offices in Topeka."

She seemed to think about the next question before asking. "Why did you leave Sarasota?"

That answer was easy. He took a swig of beer. "Because I was miserable there. Too many Floridians. Not enough flamingos."

Her lips twitched with a smile, and he relaxed a bit more. They could do this. They were mature adults who could discuss the past, even though theirs had been turbulent. Even though her breakup style had been that of the scorched earth variety. Even though half the reason he'd been so unhappy in Florida had to do with his broken heart.

"Are you seeing anyone?" she asked.

That question knocked him right back to square one, and his chest tightened. He wasn't seeing anyone, and he hadn't in nearly a year. No one significant, anyway, but that really wasn't any of Allie's business. At least not until she'd earned the answer.

"MY TURN TO ASK SOME QUESTIONS," he said. "How long did you stay in Chicago?"

She'd gotten more from him so far than she'd expected. It was only fair she did some sharing too. She definitely owed him that. She owed him complete honesty.

"I moved there about a month after you left Sandusky for Sarasota. I stayed almost three years, then I went to Glenville when my mom started getting sick."

"Were you sorry to leave Chicago?"

"Not really. It was expensive to live there. I didn't like the traffic, and the people I worked with kind of sucked. Not all of them, but enough of them to make working there difficult." Maybe she should add that for the first six months she cried pretty much every single day because she missed him so much. She'd cried after six months too. Not every day, but often enough. Some nights she'd slept with his old sweatshirt wadded up like a stuffed animal. Eventually she got tired of her own tears and decided to move forward. But every single time she'd cried, she'd wondered if breaking up with him had been a mistake. And now that question was fresh in her mind again. So much for total honesty. He wasn't necessarily ready to hear that part yet.

"Do you have a dog?" he asked, smiling ever so slightly.

"No. I don't even have any houseplants. I can't be trusted to take care of anything that's alive. I'm too forgetful. I'm not good at taking care of things."

His look turned contemplative as he paused. "You moved home to help take care of your mom. Seems like maybe you're learning how."

That was just like Dylan, to defend *her* to *herself*. Ironically, that had been one of her greatest fears about getting married. He always saw her as better than she was, and she couldn't face that moment when he figured out his loyalty had been misplaced. And so, she'd gone and proven it by saying yes, and then saying no. But still, here he was, trying to give her the benefit of the doubt.

"Maybe I am, but if you'd married me five years ago, I would've been a shitty wife."

He turned his face away to stare out the big window

of the pub for the space of a heartbeat, then turned back to her. "We'll never know what would've happened. All we know is what did happen."

"And I'm really sorry about what did happen. Do you hate me?"

"Does it seem like I hate you?" His tone was resigned, as if it would have been easier for him if he did.

"No, but you're a very nice person and maybe you're just being extra nice to me, even if I don't deserve it."

He stared at her for a moment as if measuring his words. "Why did you break up with me, Allie? I thought everything was so good with us."

A very justifiable and not unexpected question. "It was good with us. Really good, but at that time, the thought of being married terrified me. My mom gave up everything when she married my dad, and he never appreciated it. He still doesn't. She has a PhD in physics, you know, and she ended up being a stay-at-home mom because my father likes to have dinner waiting on the table when he gets home. And honestly, when she found out we were engaged, she wasn't very happy. Not because of you. She adored you, but she was worried that all that work I'd done to become a meteorologist would just take a back seat to your career."

He frowned, lines forming across his forehead. "But I'm nothing like your father. Did you think I expected you to give up everything? Did I ever treat you like less than an equal?"

"No."

No, he hadn't. Not ever. He'd treated her like a partner and a true friend. She'd just been too young and inexperienced to appreciate how rare that was. She'd thought her parents' marriage was the only kind there was. The kind where wives sacrificed everything, and husbands benefited and took you for granted.

She gave a little sigh. "I realize it doesn't sound logical now, Dylan, because we're older and hopefully wiser, but it felt like an insurmountable thing to me then. I don't blame my mom because she thought she was looking out for me, but she didn't understand I could have both a husband and a job. I guess her perspective on marriage tarnished mine, and she was pretty persuasive. Looking back, I think I finally understand that I was afraid if we got married, I wouldn't be able to live up to your expectations of marriage, and I also wouldn't be able to live up to my own expectations as a meteorologist. I was in an unwinnable situation. I know that's no excuse, but it's the only explanation I've got."

His frown gradually turned to reluctant acceptance, but she could see he was struggling with it. "We would've done okay, you know. We could've stayed together. Or had the world's longest engagement. It would've been good."

"Probably." She sighed because she agreed. "But would you have given up your job offer in Florida to follow me to Chicago? Be honest with yourself. Or would you have expected me to go with you instead?"

He shook his head, the frown returning, as if he wanted to understand her but was frustrated, nonetheless. "I don't know, Allie. You never gave me the option of making that decision. You just decided for us. It seems like something we could've talked through."

The server came and delivered their food with little fanfare. "Two homemade lasagnas, wink wink. Can I get you two another round of drinks?"

"Yes," they said in unison, breaking a bit of the tension.

Allison smiled but felt more weary than amused. "I'm sorry, Dylan. I wish I could go back and handle things differently. I can't tell you how many times I thought about calling you."

He took a swig of beer, eyeing her cautiously. "Why didn't you?"

"I don't have a good answer for that. I guess I just wanted to prove I'd made the right choice and so I threw all my energy into my job. If I couldn't have you, I wanted to at least have that."

"And do you? I mean, are you happy with your job? Was it worth it?"

He was trying to sound conversational, but there was a tone of accusation. She could feel the sense of betrayal behind his words, and no wonder. They'd left so much unsaid the night of their breakup. At the time, she'd thought she was making the right decision but had to admit, in the five years since, she'd never really stopped second-guessing herself. That had to mean something. It also had to mean something that she'd never met another person who seemed to understand her the way he did. No one who made her laugh at stupid weather jokes or coaxed her out of her comfort zone. No one who ever truly made her stop feeling lonely. Maybe that's because she wasn't actually lonely. She was just missing Dylan.

She toyed nervously with the cocktail straw in her drink and considered her answer.

"Those are two very different questions. Yes, I'm happy with my job although not completely. It's not exactly where I thought I'd be at this stage but it's the right place for now because my family needs me. And I've learned a lot over the past few years. A lot of lessons that I'm grateful for, but as far as it being worth it?" Her eyes locked with his, and her heart tumbled. "No. It wasn't worth it. No job was worth giving you up."

Her own admission surprised her and set her pulse racing. She'd never said that out loud. Not to anyone. She hadn't even allowed herself to think it until just this moment, because if leaving Dylan had been a mistake, then she'd just wasted five years of her life chasing a dream that wouldn't ever make her truly happy. Maybe it was time to reorganize her priorities, because suddenly all the things she'd thought were more important than love started fading into the distance.

Dylan stared back at her, motionless. Outside, the headlights of a passing car sent yellow beams rolling over their table. Voices from the kitchen and the other patrons melded into an indistinct hum, while a billiard ball falling into a pocket caused one player to whoop with victory while his opponent groaned in defeat. The front door opened, and an elderly couple meandered in. And Allison waited.

"Wow," Dylan said softly, calmly, after what seemed

an eternity. "Is that why you came on this trip? To tell me that?"

"No. In all honesty, I didn't even know you were a storm chaser when my news director put me on this assignment. Then I saw your name on the paperwork and nearly cancelled. I'm glad I didn't. Even if you decide you don't want anything more to do with me, I'm suddenly very glad to have told you that truth. I just wish I'd figured it out a long time ago."

"Me too." He looked down at his plate, and she could tell he was trying to process all that she'd just said. It was a lot. For her it was a huge burden lifted. The shame and regret she'd carried deep within about how she'd ended things finally started to dissipate. She was being completely honest—with herself—for the first time since he'd walked out of that restaurant five years ago with her engagement ring in his pocket.

But she knew, for Dylan, this *reunion* had been nothing but one surprise after another. He'd had no preparation, no warning, and no time to think about how he felt or what he might want to say. Just as she had with the abrupt ending of their relationship, she'd spontaneously jumped back into his life, and into his car, giving him very few options. It wasn't fair to him, but she'd make amends if he'd let her.

He took another long drink from his bottle of beer

then set it firmly on the table. He regarded her cautiously, not smiling but not *not* smiling. The frown was gone, at least. It was a step in the right direction.

"No, I'm not seeing anyone," he said quietly. "Are you?"

Her heart went whump in her chest. This was the opening she'd hoped for. "No. I've only gone on a handful of dates since we broke up. Turns out you're just about impossible to get over."

"So are you." The tension in his shoulders seemed to ease as his face relaxed into a circumspect *almost* smile.

"Well, I guess that's something we have in common then. What would you like to do about it?" She'd made far too many decisions for the two of them. This one was entirely up to Dylan.

His gaze finally warmed as it traveled over her, as if he were remembering old times and imagining new ones. Then there was a smirk. A suggestive smirk that triggered all the right stuff. "Chris is staying with Beau tonight, so I happen to have a room all to myself back at that crappy little motel. I guess the real question is, what would *you* like to do about *that*?"

Oh my. And oh, thank God. So many options, but really only one right answer, and one they both clearly wanted. "Well… we could have our waitress put this Stouffer's lasagna into a couple of take-out containers, and we could, maybe, go back to your crappy little motel room so I can show you how much I've missed you for the past five years."

He smiled fully at last, his chuckle mischievous and naughty. "I am not likely to turn down that offer." His hand shot up to signal to the server. "Check, please."

CHAPTER 9

"Slow down," Allie said breathlessly, laughing. "I can't walk as fast as you can."

They were halfway back to the motel, and he slowed his pace, but his heart kept pumping as if he were in a sprint to the finish line.

"Sorry. I'm in a hurry." His laughter joined with hers as they rushed to his room. He fumbled with the key card and hoped he could get his bearings before he made a fool of himself pawing at her. Clumsy hands were not a turn-on, and he felt the pressure to make this night one for the record books. He knew it would be for him, but he needed it to be that way for her as well.

There were more questions he wanted to ask her, of course. More things he wanted and needed to know, but all of that could wait. For now, he'd focus on enjoying every minute of removing that little flowered dress and leaving it on a heap next to his bed. He'd focus on kissing every inch of her skin just to see if she tasted as good in real life as she always did in his memories. And he'd focus on rediscovering all those little secret spots of her body that had always held such mystery for him. Pacing himself would be essential, but that was a tall order because not only had it been a while since he'd been with *anyone*, it was a lifetime since he'd been with Allie.

Two steps into the room, she turned and all but launched herself against him, pulling him in for a kiss that knocked every sense of restraint from his mind. Thank God. She was as eager as he was, and that was not something he'd take for granted. Her arms wove up around his shoulders and he hugged her tightly, reveling in the sensation of her breasts pressing against his chest. He'd missed those. A lot. He'd missed her breasts and her lips and her skin. He'd missed the curve of her back and the breathy little sounds she made when he was doing things exactly right. The mere thought of that set his blood on fire. He'd better start thinking about baseball or taxes or cloud formations or something, or else this night would end far too soon.

Allie took a few steps backward, tugging him with her toward the bed while pulling up his shirt. He laughed and pulled it over his head and let it drop to the carpet.

"Damn, woman."

She leaned back an inch and looked up at his face, her eyes bright, her cheeks already flushed with antici-pation. "Too fast?"

"Not hardly." He picked her up under her bottom and took the last few steps until they tumbled to the mattress. The headboard gave a loud wooden creak of protest, but they ignored it. If he needed to pay a secu-rity deposit for broken furniture, so be it.

ALLISON HAD PLANNED to take things slow, maybe start with a little kissing just to see if the memories held up to reality. To see if it felt *right* between them, but they'd stepped over the threshold of his crappy little motel room and suddenly she couldn't help herself and she'd jumped into his arms. Now they were wrangling on the bed, and she was tugging enthusiastically at the waist-band of his jeans while he nudged the hem of her sundress up to her waist. His hands were warm as he stroked the length of her thigh, resting his palm against her hip. Her whole body was alive and trembling. She might have felt teary with joy if she hadn't been so impatient with desire, her physical longing equal to the tender cravings in her heart.

He leaned up on his elbows to gaze down at her for so long she finally asked, "What?"

He shook his head. "Nothing, I just want to memorize you like this."

His words were meant to be an endearment, but they sounded too much like a goodbye, so she arched up and kissed him again, stopping all conversation. She needed him now, before she thought of any reasons why this might not be the best idea. She eased her mind with the knowledge that this was Dylan, the same Dylan who had always loved her well in the past. Her Dylan. At least for tonight.

Hours later, as they lay spent and satisfied in the creaky motel bed, he toyed with a strand of her hair, staring at it as if it were something magical. They were side by side, facing one another with the light from the bathroom illuminating the room just enough so they might see one another, but not so bright they couldn't doze off if the mood struck. Or in this case, if that mood *didn't* strike. Again.

The first time had been frantic and lusty, leaving them breathless, laughing with wonder, and tossing off the sheets to cool their heated skin. The second time they'd taken the scenic route and explored each other's bodies, meandering around curves and muscles, loitering over peaks and valleys until Allie thought she'd die from anticipation. Then Dylan sent her senses spiraling into blissful oblivion. Again.

"Is it my imagination or are we even better at this than we were five years ago?" she asked, tucking the motel blanket under her arms.

Dylan's chuckle came from deep in his chest. He looked adorably sleepy as he gave her a lazy smile. "I remember it always being good. Exceptionally good, but you might be right. We may have set a new standard."

She smiled back. "Pretty remarkable considering the bleak surroundings." She looked around the budget motel, taking in the bumpy stucco walls, cheap artwork, and bland color scheme.

"And the lumpy mattress and the noisy headboard," he added.

"I liked the noisy headboard. I just hope we didn't keep the neighbors awake. Please tell me none of your guys are next door."

"Okay. I won't tell you that."

A mild rush of embarrassment ran through her. "Awesome. I guess I won't worry too much about doing the walk of shame to get back to my own room then. So much for discretion."

"I think that ship sailed as soon as I asked Chris to bunk with Beau. Sorry."

Allie laughed. "Hannah told me she'd find someplace else to sleep too. I guess this cat is entirely out of the bag. I hope that doesn't make things awkward for the next few days with the crew."

Dylan rolled onto his back and pulled her with him. "I'm sure they can handle it, although you might want to prepare for some teasing. I'm sure I'll take the brunt of it, but these guys are not subtle with their humor."

"Duly noted." She snuggled a little closer. "I should probably go back to my own room, though. Don't you think? I don't want to overstay my welcome." She didn't want to leave. She wanted to stay right where she was, but it seemed polite to at least make the offer. He glanced at her, that little crease of a frown on his forehead.

"I'll walk you to your room if you want to go, but… I was kind of hoping you might stick around until morning."

She smiled. "I thought you'd never ask."

CHAPTER 10

Bright sunlight streamed in through a crack between the curtain panels, and Dylan felt Allie stir beside him. She sighed softly, still asleep, and he marveled at how the night had played out. Better than he could have imagined. He breathed in the scent of her hair and resisted the urge to wake her with a kiss. He'd let her sleep instead because they hadn't gotten much rest last night. Fortunately, the storm systems they'd be following today were not too far from their current location.

He heard the shower turn on in the room next door and tamped down a chuckle. Nathan and Rob were on the other side of that wall, and he could hear them talking. Not clearly, but well enough to know that whatever noise he and Allie had made during the night was probably not a secret. He was either going to get teased mercilessly or applauded. Or quite possibly both. Neither idea bothered him, although he didn't want them ribbing Allie too much. She could probably handle it, but he wasn't entirely sure yet how he felt about everything, and until he'd made up his mind, he didn't want his guys getting too involved.

Actually, that wasn't entirely accurate. He mostly felt amazing about what went on last night. This morning, he felt taller and stronger and smarter, like her kiss turned him into a superhero, but he knew all of that was basically pride. His ego and his body were thrilled with this latest turn of events. But his memory wasn't as happy. His memory knew what it felt like to lose her. He wasn't ready for that again, but another goodbye was practically inevitable.

The truth was Dylan loved his job. Storm chasing was an adrenaline rush, but more importantly, the information they gathered was useful. They were the front line of forecasting because no radar system, regardless of how advanced it may be, could beat human teams on the ground. Radar couldn't tell when a funnel made contact with the earth, or see the mini vortices surrounding the storm, and he knew it was those smaller funnels within that often-determined which structure was going to be demolished, and which would escape damage. He had an instinct for what he was doing, and he didn't want to give it up.

But Allie's life was in Michigan. Her family was there, and though she said her mother was improving, it sounded like they needed her. Her question last night needled at him, because when she asked if he would've given up the job offer in Sarasota to follow her to Chicago, he knew what his answer would have been: No. He wouldn't have given up his opportunity. Not at twenty-three. He would've suggested she get a job in Florida, or that perhaps they could try a long-distance relationship. He wasn't a chauvinist like her father, but five years ago, he may have thought his job was slightly more important than hers. That self-reflection made him uncomfortable and left him feeling selfish. But who was right in that situation? When you had two career-minded individuals living in different places, neither was wrong for wanting the other to relocate. Which left them at an impasse. It put them right back where they were five years ago.

ALLISON FELT the mattress shift as Dylan got up and she opened her eyes in time to see his smooth bare ass as he went into the bathroom and closed the door. She stretched like a cat and smiled into the beam of sunlight, feeling thoroughly satisfied and decadent. She grabbed her phone from the nightstand to discover a text from Hannah:

I HOPE YOU'RE PROUD OF YOURSELF, YOUNG LADY. STAYING OUT ALL NIGHT LIKE A HARLOT. YOUR FATHER AND I HAVE BEEN WORRIED SICK. JUST KIDDING. HOPE YOU HAD A GREAT NIGHT. I EXPECT A FULL REPORT. SEE YOU AT BREAKFAST.

Dylan came back out a few minutes later with a towel wrapped around his waist.

"Hey, sleepy. I was just going to jump in the shower. How are you?" He dropped a kiss onto the top of her tousled head.

"That depends," she answered, tugging on the towel. "Can you come back to bed?"

He smiled. "You have no idea how much I want to say yes but we have to get moving. Everybody else is already heading to breakfast, and this morning's forecast has some storms developing east of here. We need to get on the road."

Her disappointment was probably out of proportion to the circumstances, but she had a nagging sensation that last night might have been their only night. At least during this week. And maybe for good. She had no idea what the future would hold, and she wanted to spend as much time with him as she could.

"Do you think…" She let the question linger because she didn't dare ask.

He sat down on the bed. "Do I think what?"

"Do you think we have a chance?" she whispered, as if saying it too loudly would tempt the fates, and not in their favor.

"Do you want us to have a chance?" He wove his fingers in with hers.

"Do you?"

His sigh came from deep down, and her heart preemptively began to ache.

When he spoke, his voice was slow and thoughtful. "Do you remember how you felt yesterday when you stood and watched that massive tornado?"

She nodded, not sure where this was headed as he continued, still looking down at their entwined hands. "When I see a storm like that, I'm captivated. I know it's powerful enough to annihilate me, but I'm fascinated anyway. I'm always torn by wanting to get closer and closer but knowing how dangerous it is. Sometimes I take risks that I regret later, and other times I remember to be more careful. And sometimes I rush in, and it all pays off."

He looked up and into her eyes. "Allie, that's how you make me feel. Still, even after all these years. Everything I feel for you is dangerous and risky and powerful, and I can't lie. I don't want to get hurt again. Not like last time. You nearly destroyed me. I don't know what the payoff would be if we tried again because even if you have all good intentions now, we live in two different cities. Two different states, even. We each have our own jobs, our own careers, and they don't currently overlap. I don't know what to do about that."

All the warm, happy buzz from last night was replaced with a strong dose of stark, harsh reality. She knew he was right. Their lives didn't intersect. She couldn't expect him to uproot his world to work around hers, and she had her own obligations and plans that kept her in Michigan. Saddest of all, she knew she'd made it hard for him to trust her with his heart. She might still love him, and he might even still love her... but sometimes love just wasn't enough.

Her sigh matched his. Deep and heavy. "I don't know what to do about it either. I guess all I can ask is if maybe we try to make the most of these next couple of days? I don't want to crowd you or make things awkward for the rest of this week, but I want you to know, Dylan, if last night is all we get, I'm still really happy to have had this time with you."

She meant that with all her heart, but even as she said the words, she knew, deep down, that those few hours they'd just shared weren't nearly enough for her. Now that he was back in her life, she wanted to keep him there. She didn't want this week to be about closing an old chapter of her life. She wanted it to be the beginning of an entirely new story. But how?

"I like that idea," he said, nodding slowly. "We'll make the most of this week and then"—he pressed a soft kiss against her bare shoulder—"then we'll talk again before you leave. Let's not put a lot of pressure on figuring things out right now. Especially because you've got me all confused and... I don't know. I can't really think straight when I know you're naked under that sheet."

She laughed, but he silenced her with a kiss that sent her senses spinning. And when he pressed her back against the bed, she laughed again.

"Isn't everybody waiting for us?" she asked, pushing the covers aside to grant him more access to her body.

"They can wait," he murmured against her throat.

She sighed with relief and kissed him back. A few days from now they might have to say goodbye, but for now, this would have to be enough.

CHAPTER 11

"I don't know about the rest of you," Chris said loudly to the group as Dylan and Allie finally walked into the diner for breakfast, "but I detect a distinct change in the atmosphere around here. A frost warning has been averted."

Hannah nodded, staring pointedly at Allie. "Is it possible that storm clouds have made way for sunny skies?"

"Okay, okay," Dylan said, chuckling. "Everybody get it all out of your systems. All the jokes at once so we can move on, and let's remember we're all professionals here. And adults."

"I am barely an adult," Nathan answered. "And I heard stuff last night that I cannot unhear. I think I deserve some hazard pay for that."

Allie's cheeks turned crimson, and she ducked her head, letting her hair fall over her face as she turned toward Dylan. With his arm around her waist, he could feel her silent laughter. The ribald comments continued while everyone shuffled around adjusting chairs so Dylan and Allie could join them at the table. Somewhere during the commentary, she was dubbed *Tornado Allie*, while they, as a couple, were christened *Dyllison*. No one, fortunately, questioned their history and better yet, no one questioned their future. It was just good-natured ribbing and Dylan felt a surge of gratitude because the underlying message from his crew—his friends—was all positive.

As the rest of the week progressed, the group shifted into a subtle new routine. By day, they'd chase storms, stopping for Allie to do her segments, and even managing a couple of live reports including one with a stovepipe funnel cloud touching down in the background right behind her. Meanwhile, Dylan and Chris and their crew captured a fair amount of useful data and aided Channel 17 with some on the spot reporting. Professionally, it was a great stretch of severe weather. The kind they lived for.

At the end of the day, they'd have dinner as a group at some mom-and-pop dive, and then came Dylan's favorite part. The time when he and Allie would head off to their own room and pretend that everything was going to be just fine. Dingy motel rooms with squeaky beds and questionable soundproofing became their temporary oasis from the world outside. During those luscious midnight hours, he showed her all the ways that he still loved her, even though he never said it. And neither did she. They both knew it was unspoken, but also recognized that saying the words out loud would only complicate matters. He tried, and failed, to keep his heart from the equation, knowing she had to go home at the end of the week.

On Saturday, the weather turned particularly fierce, spawning no less than two dozen funnel clouds stretching from one end of Tornado Alley to the other. They followed one intense wedge for several miles until downed power lines across the only access road left them trapped in a tiny Oklahoma town that had suffered considerable damage just an hour earlier.

"The mayor states an early warning system gave residents time to find shelter and there are currently no reported injuries," Hannah said, reading the news story from her phone as Chris carefully pulled the Blaster into a grocery store parking lot littered with broken tree branches and other debris. Nathan parked next to him with the Sidewinder and soon the crew was gathered outside the vehicles with everyone surveying the surrounding damage. The front awning of a hardware store dangled precariously from the roofline. An uprooted tree had demolished the tiny coffee shop next to it, and several other shops were all but flattened into piles of kindling. This was a part of the job Dylan would never get used to, the human toll in the storm's aftermath. Allie came to stand beside him, her face etched with sadness and disbelief.

"These poor families," she said. "So much destruction. Oh my gosh. Look at that."

He followed her gaze and across the debris-littered street stood what was left of a tiny country church. The entire front wall and much of the roof was now missing. The steeple lay on the ground, but the pale stone altar and the back wall full of windows remained. And standing on the front steps was a cluster of tuxedo-clad men and a minister.

"Holy shit, it's a wedding party," Hannah said, instantly lifting up her camera.

ALLISON LIFTED HER HAND, halting Hannah. "Let's get their permission before doing any filming. I don't want to be insensitive. Hopefully, they'd like to talk to us, though." It was a fine line between reporting a story and exploiting a situation, and she wanted to be on the right side of that. The crew followed as she made her way through the rubble with Dylan close to her side.

"Is everyone okay?" he called out as they got closer.

The men turned in unison. They were various ages and sizes, with one man markedly older than the rest. Most of them shared a notable family resemblance.

"We're okay," answered the tallest man. He had dark hair and a neatly trimmed beard. "Y'all with the news?"

"I am," Allison answered. "I'm Allison Winters with Channel 7 News in Glenville, Michigan. We don't want to intrude but if you don't mind sharing, I'd like to hear about your experience."

He nodded and stepped forward. "Sure thing. I'll tell you all about it. I'm supposed to get married in this church today." He pointed over his shoulder with his thumb. "Guess I'm glad it didn't fall down when we were all inside."

"I'm so sorry for your troubles," Allison said. "Would you mind if we talked to you on film?"

His suddenly broad smile seemed out of place, given the circumstances. "Sure thing. Can we go grab my bride? She'd get a real kick out of being on TV and so far, it hasn't been the best day."

"Absolutely." Allison nodded at Hannah who

instantly started filming. They'd get as much raw
footage as possible and tighten things up in editing.
"Where is she?"

"Over here." He gestured for them to follow as he
and the rest of his dazed and bewildered groomsmen
walked behind what was left of the church. The back
part of the building seemed to be untouched by damage.
He opened a steel door and called inside.

"Mariska! Hey, Sugar Bear. We got news people
out here. Want to be on TV?"

Seconds later a short, round bride in an audaciously
frou-frou dress appeared in the doorway. He took her
hand and helped her step outside. She was half his
height, even with a four-inch monstrosity of a veil on
top of her black hair, and in spite of the dismal situation, she too had the biggest, brightest smile. Allison
found herself smiling back at this defiantly happy
couple.

"TV? Why sure. I'd love to be on TV. Wait until my
sister hears about this. That'll teach her to skip my
wedding just because of a little tornado warning."

Allison gathered some basic information before
suggesting they return to the front steps of the church
to film the actual segment. She wanted the destruction
of the building as a backdrop to the story. She wasn't
particularly religious, but even she recognized that the

symbolism of the pristine altar, standing untouched amid all that destruction, couldn't be missed.

"Just be natural," she said to the couple once they were standing where the doors should have been. "Please start with your names and then tell me anything you'd like to share about today."

As they spoke, the wedding party and several guests gathered around, along with the rest of Dylan's crew and a smattering of other bystanders. There were bridesmaids in sparkly turquoise gowns, the minister wearing a white collar smudged with dirt, and a weeping mother of the bride who kept a lace hanky pressed to her mouth to stifle her sobs. She was visibly, and understandably, distressed but the rest of the attendants were stoic and probably in a bit of shock.

"I'm Remi Martinez," said the groom. "And this is my bride, Mariska Garcia. We were getting pictures taken before the ceremony, and doing them in shifts, on account of Mariska didn't want me to see her before the wedding. Me and the guys were in the chapel when we heard the sirens go off. I could already hear the wind start to howl, and let me tell you, superstitions aside, nothing was going to keep me from getting to my Sugar Bear."

Mariska's sparkly eyes welled with tears as she gazed up at him lovingly and clutched his brawny arm.

He got a little misty, too, pulling the silk pocket square from his tuxedo jacket and dabbing at his eyes. "I sure as heck wasn't about to hunker down for a tornado until I knew she was safe, so all us guys high-tailed it to the back where the gals were. I grabbed on to her tight, and we waited out the storm."

By now even more of a crowd had gathered to observe what was happening, with everyone listening intently even while the sound of chain saws hummed in the distance as rescue crews began the arduous task of cleanup.

"He sure did grab on tight," Mariska added. "I could hardly breathe but even when we heard the front of the church falling, I knew everything would be okay. Remi always takes such good care of me, and I can't wait to be married. Guess that'll have to wait though." She glanced back at the church, the first hint of sadness passing over her face.

"We were supposed to get married at four o'clock today." Remi nodded, gazing over at his fiancée. He paused for the space of a heartbeat before adding, "And I say let's do it. Sugar Bear, I know this isn't the day you'd planned, but we've got the preacher here. What do you think about making it legal right now? Right here on the steps?"

The bride gasped, but her joy was obvious and

instantaneous, and Allison felt her own breath hitch at the sweetly romantic gesture. A murmur of surprise and encouragement rippled through the collection of guests as Mariska cast a glance back toward what was left of the modest little church. Remnants of wedding flowers and silk ribbons were scattered about amid dust and debris, but the afternoon sun shone brightly through the handful of stained-glass windows that remained, creating a kaleidoscope over the mess. If you squinted a little, it looked kind of pretty. Mariska must've thought so too, because she turned back and grinned at Remi as she offered up a taffeta-rustling shrug. "Happily ever after, here we come!" she said.

Allison cast a smile directly at Hannah's camera. This wasn't her typical weather report, but certainly the news director back at Channel 7 was going to love it. A little drama, a little resilience in the face of adversity, a little bit of a love story. It had all the elements of a really great segment, plus it was just plain adorable. Allison caught Dylan's eye and could tell he was thinking the same thing. And from his expression, she suspected that he was also thinking about *them*, and a wedding that should've happened but never did. She should fix that.

"You kids want to get married right now?" the minister asked, and for a second, Allison thought he was talking to her. Her cheeks flushed, and Dylan chuckled.

"We do," the bride and groom said.

"Right now," Mariska added, clearly not interested in taking any chances on another postponement.

There was a bit of jostling and strategic rearranging as the wedding attendants moved to take their places, and Allison took her cue to step aside. She joined Dylan just a few feet away from the bride and groom. Hannah and Rob kept filming as someone played the wedding march from their cell phone, and the bride's mother never stopped crying.

The ceremony was brief, in part because, as the minister explained, "The good Lord saw fit to blow all my notes away, so you'll have to bear with me. We'll make this one a quickie." He mentioned all the standard things about loving and cherishing, and Dylan slid his hand into Allison's giving it a squeeze that went straight to her heart.

"And as we're gathered here today to celebrate the marriage of these two fine people," the preacher added, "always remember this: When life's storms come your way—and they will—grab on tight to the people you love and don't let ever go. Don't ever take a moment of sunshine for granted and believe that above all else a rainbow of hope is always on the horizon."

An hour later, under a white tent hastily re-erected by a collection of strangers, the reception caterers set up a buffet line to feed whomever was nearby: family members, wedding guests, rescue crews. The newly-weds welcomed everyone, and a glowing sense of unity and celebration prevailed. It was magical for all of its simplicity, and the storm-chasing crew filled their plastic solo cups to toast the bride and groom more than once. Allison was feeling mildly tipsy, and overwhelmingly sentimental. It was no wonder, what with all the love in the air. She couldn't help it.

Dylan came over and sat down next to her, handing her a paper plate piled high with pink frosted wedding cake, and held up two plastic forks.

"Feel like sharing?" he asked.

"I do," she said, smiling at her own brazen innuendo.

Dylan chuckled but said nothing.

They ate the cake, watching as Remi and Mariska danced in the grass to the sound of more cell phone–provided music, and Allison sighed thoughtfully. This could have been her and Dylan if she'd never given him that ring back. Not the tornado part, or the demolished church, of course, but they could have been a happy couple facing the future together, knowing they'd always have each other to depend on during those life-storms the preacher talked about. Maybe it was time for her to do some grabbing on tight.

She turned to Dylan. "You know that stuff the minister said about hope always being on the horizon? And not taking any sunny moments for granted?"

"Yeah." Dylan nodded slowly, not looking her way until she took ahold of his hand. When his eyes met hers, she felt utterly vulnerable but thoroughly optimistic by the warmth in his gaze.

"Well," she said, "I guess I should tell you… I'm pretty sure I'm in love with you again. Honestly, I'm not sure I ever stopped. I don't know what to do about it, but I'm entirely positive I want you in my life. If you'll have me, I promise I'll never break your heart again."

A smile tilted the corners of his mouth ever so slightly, as if he were fighting it. "Are you sure that's not just the wedding vibes talking? Maybe all the matrimony in the atmosphere has you light-headed and confused?"

She sensed the teasing in his tone and smiled. "I'm not confused. Maybe for the first time in a long time I'm absolutely certain of what I want. I love you. Maybe it's like *The Wizard of Oz*, you know? It took a tornado to teach me that all I ever really needed was what I'd had all along. You're all I need, Dylan. There are lots of news stations and lots of jobs. We'll figure something out. If you still want me."

He stared at her for so long she thought, for a disastrous moment, that he might not think she was worth the effort. Maybe he hadn't forgiven her after all, but then he smiled, and all was right with the world again.

He pulled one of her hands to his lips and gave it a kiss. "Allie, after being together during these past couple of days, I'm not sure I could give you up again. Turns out I never stopped loving you either. I tried but... I just love you. Rain or shine."

She reached up and pressed her palm against his cheek. "I love you too. Rain or shine. And if I catch Sugar Bear's bouquet, you might just have to marry me."

EPILOGUE
SIX MONTHS LATER...

"Hey, isn't that my sweatshirt?" Dylan asked as Allie climbed into bed beside him. "I thought I'd lost that thing years ago."

She smiled. "It is yours. I used to sleep with it in Chicago on nights when I was really missing you." She tried to nudge Judy toward the end of the bed, but the oversized dog wasn't budging. It had been a month since Dylan transferred to the Michigan branch of the weather service and moved in with her, but she and the dog were still working out their jealousy issues and trying to establish who got to sleep the closest to him. So far, the dog was winning.

Dylan snapped his fingers and Judy relented, casting a doleful glance at Allie.

"Well, the good news is," he said. "Now that I live

here in Glenville, you'll never have to miss me. So, you can give it back."

Allie shook her head as she adjusted the pillows behind her. "Sorry, I'm never giving it back. It's mine now but you can wear it sometimes if you want to."

He eyed her for a moment with a frown that was not at all menacing. "I think that promotion of yours has made you awfully sassy." Then his smile turned mischievous. "But maybe we could work out a trade. I have something of yours that I've been meaning to give back."

"Really? What?" She plumped up the pillows behind her again, trying to get comfortable, and pushing against the dog with her foot to no avail.

Dylan twisted to the side and opened the drawer of the nightstand, fumbling around for a moment. Then he turned back to her, his smile now adoring and sweet. Her heart gave a little skip as he held out a closed fist, and slowly opened it to reveal a tiny black velvet box. He reached out with the other hand and popped it open, and there was her engagement ring. He'd saved it all this time. Allie's breath cut short in her throat, and she blinked in elated disbelief.

"Allie, I love you, rain or shine," he said, his voice husky with emotion. "I was wondering if you might want this back. But I should warn you, I come with it.

If you want the ring, you have to marry me. Like, actually marry me this time."

Tears sprang to her eyes, and joy filled her heart. "You know I'll probably be a lousy wife, right? I'm a terrible cook and I can't even take care of a houseplant."

Dylan nodded. "Yep, I know. But you're everything I want. I think you're damn near perfect, and anyway, even if you're a lousy wife, you'll always be the best meteorologist I've ever worked with."

Like a rainbow after the storm, Allie could see nothing but happiness on the horizon. There were a million things she wanted to say to him. A million ways she wanted to express her love, but words couldn't capture all that she felt.

So, she said the only thing that mattered.

"In that case… yes. Yes, yes, yes, yes, yes. And yes."

THE END

PREVIEW: ART OF THE CHASE

Want more from Tracy Brogan?
Read on for a preview of Art of Chase, the first book in
Tracy's new series The Bostwicks of Trillium Bay.

CHAPTER 1

TRILLIUM BAY, 1888

C harles David Bostwick was a grown man. A serious man blessed with an innate intellect – thanks to his superior parentage – and a brilliant head for business – thanks in no small measure to his very fine, very expensive, East Coast education. The highest echelons of Chicago society considered him to be both charmingly handsome and exceedingly capable – even while acknowledging that by all accounts *he* also found himself to be both handsome and capable. Yet no one could deny that Charles Bostwick was a man of lofty ambitions and inevitable success. Indeed. The man had finesse. He had panache. He had *plans*.

Yet nowhere in the breadth or depth of his wildest dreams could Charles Bostwick have foreseen how his finely tuned plans could be so unceremoniously waylaid by two long-bodied, stubby legged dogs – although calling them *dogs* put an even further strain on his imagi-nation – and he himself was the very picture of ridicu-lousness walking them down Main Street of Trillium Bay clutching their delicate leashes – leashes made of made of ribbon, no less! Pink, grosgrain ribbon tied in petite bows around the neck of each wee mutt.

It was an utter humiliation to be strolling in public with two such unappealing creatures, not to mention doing so during a torrential downpour that left rain streaming from the brim of his bowler hat. An umbrella would be a fine thing just now, but he'd left the Imperial Hotel in such haste he hadn't bothered to check the sky and now it was too late. He looked the fool with every aspect of the situation injurious to his pride. Especially since he *should be* working right now. He should be at his desk – in his office – in *Chicago*! But no. He was here, all but marooned on this tiny resort island off the coast of northern Michigan.

And all because of just fourteen damnable minutes.

Fourteen minutes, a mere 840 seconds that had forever relegated him to being *the second son*. He could have been the first born, but thanks to fate or destiny or midwifery malpractice, Alexander had come first. Alex, his twin brother in looks if not in temperament, had come forth into this world at 4:08 p.m. with a smile and a coo *(or so the story went)* while he himself had loitered in the womb for nearly another quarter of an hour and arrived on his own schedule at 4:22 p.m. with a scowl and a squall. It was *the longest quarter of an hour* of his mother's entire existence *(according to her)*, and he'd spent much of his life trying to make that up to her – and to catch up, if only figuratively, with his *older* brother. Throughout childhood, such was his fervor to be first whenever possible, his family had all but abandoned calling him Charles and instead, called him Chase.

Intellectually, he knew none of this should trouble him anymore. He'd proven himself his brother's equal – if not superior – in virtually every way, and in truth was far more like their father than Alex was. But of late, the old sibling rivalry had been gnawing at him again – because it was Alex who had recently become engaged. And because it was Alex's future son who would one day carry the family moniker of Alexander James Bostwick – *the Third*. And because, if Chase were being brutally honest with himself, he was upset because it was his brother who was engaged to none other than Isabella Carnegie.

She was a distant cousin to *those* Carnegies, but it wasn't her wealth or societal connections that made her so appealing a bride. No, it was something much simpler. Isabella Carnegie was a true beauty with thick blonde tresses and cornflower blue eyes that appeared innocent one moment and sultry the next, causing every single young man who looked upon her to dream of marriage – and causing every settled husband to dream of being single.

And – in yet another wicked twist of happenstance – Chase had missed out on the opportunity of her by mere moments. Because he'd been *working*. Delayed by a business matter, he'd arrived late to the Kimball's annual St. Valentine's Day dinner party and Alex had met Isabella first.

Had Chase himself arrived on time and captured her in conversation first, he felt certain he could have wooed and won her, and did, in fact, try. He'd paid her a call the very next afternoon and had sent a robust arrangement of yellow jasmine in honor of her elegance and grace only to discover that Alex had already been to visit (*in the morning!*) and had been so very bold as to arrive with pink Camellias (*in hand!*) to indicate his longing. Alex may as well have shown up with an engagement ring and a preacher for all his lack of subtlety. When, a mere three weeks later, Alex confided that he and Isabella had come to an understanding, all Chase could do was shake his brother's hand and congratulate him for finding such a lovely, well-tempered bride.

That had been nearly four months ago and the whole incident had left Chase with a bruised heart. Or perhaps it was his ego? He wasn't entirely sure. Regardless, it put him off the idea of matrimony for now. He had plenty of time to find a wife. He was only twenty-five and right now work was his passion, his true mistress – not that he was ever in want for female companionship. Aside from the bevy of eager debutantes vying for his attention – and his proposal – he had a recurring appointment with a lovely young widow whose company he enjoyed very much. The casual (*and very discreet*) arrangement suited them both and neither wished to take it beyond the bedroom.

And, of course, there were the lonely wives of *other* men who occasionally sought him out – not that a gentleman would ever kiss and tell – but other than his infatuation for Isabella Carnegie, he'd yet to feel the pull to find a wife of his own.

For Chase, work was not a replacement – it was his preference, especially since he knew his father relied on him, so much more so than he relied upon Alex because, quite simply, Chase worked harder. His business instincts had proven to be both bold and lucrative while

Alex was prone to error and more of a *let's try this and see what happens* kind of operative.

So, it was an unexpected blow to Chase's pride when A.J. Bostwick, Sr. consigned *him* to the role of chaperone to *Mrs.* A.J. Bostwick while she summered at the Imperial Hotel on Wenniway Island along with the youngest Bostwick offspring, Chase's sister, Daisy. The assignment wasn't quite the same humiliation as walking these dogs but three months of involuntary captivity catering to his wearisome mother and boisterous little sister made this island more purgatory than paradise. The whole arrangement left Chase feeling... diminished. Banished. Punished somehow although his father had assured him it was no such thing.

"I need Alex in Chicago, son, so I'm relying on you. I know I can trust you to handle things on the island and, quite frankly, your mother needs looking after," A.J. had said with a hearty slap on the shoulder and the offer of a fine cigar.

While Chase wasn't prone to questioning his father's judgment, on this matter, he felt entirely certain A.J. was mistaken. Constance Bostwick did not need anyone looking after her. His mother was as rugged as a badger, running the family with steely resolve from a velvet settee. Prison wardens displayed a warmer countenance than she, but a recent bout of influenza had left her with a lingering cough, and it was decided a few months away from the soot and stink of downtown Chicago might restore her health to its typical vigor. Thus, plans were made to visit Trillium Bay and Chase was consigned to play nursemaid.

Lately though he'd begun to suspect his mother's cough was more a clever ploy than a real health concern since she'd informed him that very morning of her desire to have a summer cottage constructed on the island. She'd tried to play off the idea as a spontaneous thing, a whimsical notion or a passing thought, but Chase knew nothing his mother ever did was spontaneous. She was as calculating as a politician. She'd probably never even had the flu at all. She'd probably decided months ago that she needed a way to lure them here for a season to give her time to plot and plan.

"Well, it's not Newport, of course, but it is closer to Chicago so I suppose one must make do," she'd said to him just an hour prior. "Tomorrow you must hire a carriage and we'll tour all the available properties. I've heard the Pullmans are building here, as well as the O'Douls and the Cahills, and I know for a fact that Breezy VonMeisterburger has her eye on a spot near the west bluff. We must see it posthaste, before her husband has a chance to make an offer."

"Isn't Breezy VonMeisterburger your dearest

friend?" he'd asked, more as a reminder to his mother rather than an actual query.

She'd gazed back at him with a well-practiced air of guilelessness that might have been convincing had he not known her so well.

"She's my *closest* friend, not my dearest. There's a difference. But either way, as my friend, it would be selfish of her to claim the most coveted location before we've even had a chance to see it."

Chase knew there was no point in arguing with logic such as that, and not much point in arguing with her moments later when she'd told him to walk her precious little dogs either, which is how he now found himself trudging along in the rain behind two soggy, long-haired dachshunds and feeling rather sorry for himself. He wasn't prone to self-pity, but his wool suit was wet and beginning to itch, the dogs seemed disinclined to do their business, his brother was engaged to the most beautiful girl Chase had ever seen, and it would be weeks – months, actually – before he could return to Chicago and get on with *his life*. He was already bored with this island, and they'd only been there for four days. Four days!

Never was a man more ill-suited for relaxation than Chase Bostwick.

He knew he was the exception rather than the rule.

Thanks to fast, sleek steamships and miles upon miles of new railroad lines simplifying travel, Trillium Bay was fast-becoming a holiday mecca for wealthy, city-weary patrons, but Chase wasn't weary of the city. He loved the hustle and bustle of Chicago, the crush of people moving with purpose toward their destination, the ever-present cacophony of voices and hoofbeats and construction, the pungent aromas sweetened by robust breezes off the lake, and above all else – quite literally – the brand-new buildings so miraculously tall they were called *skyscrapers*.

Yes, he loved his city. He didn't *need* a vacation, and he didn't *want* a vacation with its string of lazy days providing him with nothing to do but sail and play lawn tennis and wonder if his brother had yet to slide a hand up under Isabella Carnegie's skirts. An improper curiosity to have about one's soon-to-be sister-in-law to be sure. He did realize that and admonished himself for the thought, but that was precisely why he needed to be working. He needed a distraction. Any kind of distraction.

Crossing the street, his foot sank into a puddle in the middle of the muddy road, and he didn't even bother to flinch or lament the ruination of his shoe or worry that anyone noticed. The whole day was turning into one big metaphorical puddle anyway, and the only saving grace of this pelting rain was that all the other poor souls out on the street right now were keeping their heads lowered, their vision shielded by black umbrellas.

Perhaps that's why she didn't see him, and why he didn't see her.

Or perhaps it was because one little dog in his charge tried to avoid the next puddle by dashing ahead while the other little dog dove into it nose-first and their leashes got tangled and intertwined as they bolted hither and yon, and the rain was drip, drip, dripping from the brim of his hat and blowing right into his eyes. Perhaps it was because thunder rumbled ominously overhead just as a flash of lightning brightened everything with the brilliance of the sun, blinding him for the length of a blink, or perhaps it was due to the sudden surge of people disembarking from the ferry and streaming into the street en masse like a flock of honking geese.

Whatever the cause, she didn't see him, and he didn't see her. Until it was too late. Suddenly, there she was, colliding with him, getting her feet twisted up in the pink ribbon leashes with the dogs barking and leaping against her dark blue skirts. She swayed intimately against him for the space of a heartbeat, and somehow the bulk of whatever she carried in her arms was knocked free and crashed with a squelchy thud upon the soaked ground and pieces flew every which way. It happened so fast, yet Chase's mind was quick to register this as an unfortunate mishap while not quite a catastrophe.

"Oh, my goodness! You nincompoop!" she cried out, shoving at his chest which naturally caused his arms to move, which only served to tighten the noose of the leashes now wound around her calves. She teetered precariously against him once more and her face twisted with a look of surprised dismay before she fell backwards onto the road – and into the mud.

Now it was a catastrophe.

"Oh!" she exclaimed again, fists clenching against her legs as she sat on the ground, rain pelting her. "Look what you've done!"

He wasn't sure if she was talking to him or the dogs – because he felt quite certain that she was the real culprit behind this blunder. Nonetheless, he was involved *and* holding on to the leashes from which the woman, a mere slip of a girl, really, was now trying to extricate her dainty ankles.

"I'm dreadfully sorry, miss," he said magnanimously, offering his hand to help the clumsy girl up. Surely the first order of business was to get her off her bustle and back onto her feet.

She spared him only the flicker of a glance, long enough for him to be certain she had dark eyes and wasn't very old. Eighteen? Twenty perhaps? It was hard to ascertain due to the scowl and the rain and her rather unfashionable hat.

She ignored his hand and instead rolled to her knees and began gathering up the items she'd dropped, seemingly indifferent to the mud – a rather unladylike reaction, in his opinion. Almost shocking. There seemed to be a wooden box in pieces around her, the base in one spot and the top in another, and around that lots of sliver tubes and little pots that, as the rain hit, splashed with colors.

It was a painter's box, he realized as he tightened the ribbon leashes around his fists trying to regain control of the dogs while bending to help her retrieve her items, but the hounds were eager to make friends, and this just served to incite them more.

"Oh!" she gasped again as one licked her face.

"Flossie, stop!" he commanded although the dog paid no heed. "Heel."

Flossie did not heel, and Chase resorted to scooping up the soggy mutts, one under each arm which rendered him useless in helping her. The dogs squirmed for their freedom, and he tightened his grip, wondering if perhaps he would be justified in squeezing them until they fainted. He wouldn't, of course. He actually liked dogs. Just not *these* dogs.

"I am sorry," he said again, meaning it sincerely because regardless of the cause of the accident *(It was her. She was the cause.)* here was a damsel in true distress and he was failing quite miserably in coming to her aid. It made him feel uncharacteristically inept. *Damn these dogs.*

Suddenly they were surrounded by people, each reaching out a hand to help the girl, some retrieving the items or pieces of the box, and one burly young man in a denim trousers and cotton shirt so well-worn that Chase could barely tell it had once been plaid lifted her about the waist and set her on her feet, not seeming to realize the abuse of his familiarity, but the girl gave him a tremulous yet grateful smile.

Well... damn again. Chase would have helped her up if not for the dogs and he vowed silently to never walk them again. They could pee on the rugs at the hotel for all he cared.

A few others handed the young woman items, and she tucked them into the box. Everything was soiled and the continued rain blended the random paints together until they too were the color of mud as it splashed on her dress and her gloves. Thunder rumbled once more followed seconds later by a lightning flash and the good Samaritans scattered, leaving just Chase, the girl, and the denim-clad man.

"Best to get under cover, Miss," Chase heard the man say while handing her the final piece of the lid. "If you bring that box to the hardware store, Davey will fix it up for you. I can take you there now, if you'd like. I'd be happy to."

She set the wooden pieces on top, holding her bundle together with both hands, and shook her dark, damp, ill-hatted head.

"Thank you, but no. I'm in a rush to get to the Imperial Hotel. They were expecting me two days ago. Can you tell me which way it is?"

"I'll see you to the Imperial," Chase said, stepping forward, determined to reestablish himself as someone useful. He was a *Bostwick*, after all. "I'll secure us a carriage and deliver you safely to the front door."

The girl looked at him warily, anger flaring in those dark eyes, as if *he* were the sole cause of this unfortunate event yet he was still fairly certain it was *she* who'd plowed into *him*. It was she who'd shoved him in the chest causing herself to tumble to the ground. Not that a gentleman would ever say as much.

"It's the very least I can do," he added. "It seems I owe you a painter's box as well." He nodded at the cargo she held tightly to chest. Whatever his role in the matter (*walking down the street, minding his own business*), he'd fix this. And since the box appeared decades old, she'd come out all the better on the other side. A new artist's box would be far superior to that dinged up antique she clutched. Perhaps she'd even consider the whole mishap an unexpected blessing.

"There's no replacing this painter's box," the young woman said, her quiet voice cracking slightly with emotion. "It was my father's. But I'll accept a carriage if it'll get me out of the rain and to the hotel."

CHAPTER 2

This was an inauspicious start to the new life Emerson Joan McKenna hoped to create for herself – although, all things considered, not that shocking. Nothing had gone well for her in quite some time, and this latest unpleasantry would simply have to be dealt with in the same manner in which she'd dealt with nearly everything else of late – with grit and denial.

Over the past several months, her life had shifted seismically from comfortably predictable to thoroughly precarious, and only recently had she concluded that flailing in an abyss of "why me?" got her nowhere. Looking back was a trap of torment, a doorway leading to nothing but melancholy and regret so now, all she could do was look forward and hope and pray her circumstances would improve, although hope was a fickle friend on whom she could not rely. She wasn't exactly on good terms with prayer, either.

She kept tossing requests upward, hoping the good Lord might overlook her past misdeeds, but lately it seemed His responses were more mercurial than ever. Even for God. While He'd graciously seen fit to prevent her steamship from sinking to the bottom of Lake Michigan on its journey from Chicago to Wenniway Island, He *had* sent the storm in the first place – a storm so severe it pitched that ship to and fro until every passenger onboard was either green with illness or white with fear. Or somehow both.

In addition to causing fright and seasickness, the foul weather delayed her arrival to the island by two full days, which made her late to the start of her recently acquired position of artist in residence at the Imperial Hotel. While her new employer would likely forgive her tardiness *(she could hardly be held responsible for bad weather, after all)*, she knew – unequivocally – that there were other things about her person of which the management might be less tolerant, so it was essential – imperative, even – that she make an excellent first impression, but arriving wet and bedraggled in a soiled dress with her hair in knots was not the stuff of good impressions!

Oh, but good gracious! How on earth was she to clean herself up? Her skirts were so stained with mud that even this hearty rain could not wash it all away. The wind had torn all but the most secure pins from her hair, and her shoes were heavy with muck. Cleaning them to a respectable appearance would take a stiff brush and more time than she had. She needed lodging to change into one of her few other gowns, gowns that were still in a trunk on the steamship, but she couldn't check into her hotel room without announcing her arrival in this current state of deshabille. A conundrum, indeed.

But those aspects of this situation were trifles compared to the distress she felt over the demolition of her father's art box. It was her greatest treasure, the only tangible thing of him she had left. The only thing that hadn't been stolen – along with her heart – and now both were irreparably damaged – and all because she'd been, once more, distracted by a handsome face.

Heaven, help her. Had she learned nothing from her past? Didn't she know that men were naught but the source of trial and strife? Wasn't this latest blunder more verifiable proof? She had places to be and work to do yet one glimpse of a tall, attractive man with droplets of water clinging to his sculpted, clean-shaven face was all it took to blind her (*yes, completely blind her*) to the dachshunds at his feet and the next thing she knew, she'd stepped right into a tangled web of leashes and paws and a chest so solid it was like slamming into a brick building. She'd bounced off that man's torso, dropped her art box, and landed right on her bum in the mud, ruining her second-best dress.

She was the nincompoop. This was her fault for not watching where she stepped – although she'd never admit it. Besides, the man should have had better control over those furry little monsters. Honestly, how difficult was it to wrangle a couple of miniscule lap dogs? At present, they remained tucked under each of his thick arms, but the dogs continued to wriggle like fish on hooks and their apparent eagerness to be free coupled with his expression of intense consternation made a comical picture indeed. She could not have drawn a caricature more absurd, but she was not in the mood for comedy. Especially since she wasn't certain if his palpably growing frustration was because of her, or the dogs. She *had* shoved him rather firmly in the sternum, but in truth, her wrists probably hurt more than his ribs.

And surely neither were more bruised than her dignity.

Nonetheless, she'd just agreed to climb into a carriage with this fortress of a man and his dainty little dogs for a ride that was sure to be awkward. She would never have agreed to it if not for her dress getting wetter – and heavier – by the moment and her desperate desire to get off the street. She had no idea how far the walk to the Imperial Hotel would be, and she most certainly could not afford a carriage for herself. Though she was loathe to admit it, quite frankly, she couldn't refuse the charity.

Ah, charity. What a detestable word. What a labyrinth of emotion it evoked because, as she now understood, help offered *freely* was often anything but charitable. There was always a price. Always a catch. Always strings attached, and if she wasn't careful, she'd end up owing this man more than she was prepared to pay. Perhaps she *should* walk to the hotel after all, no matter the distance. But thunder crashed, and lightning flashed, and Jo decided this was a risk she needed to take.

With some scrambling and assistance from the helpful worker in the plaid shirt, Jo found herself sitting across from the impeccably dressed man in a well-appointed carriage with the two wet, pink-leashed she-devils now resting quietly on the floor. She held the remnants of her art box on her lap and used the back of one gloved hand to brush the raindrops from her cheeks. Lord above, she must be a sight. And there *he* was, damp as she yet somehow looking far less worse for wear, his stiff collar not suffering for the rain, and the brown of his suit hardly showing any moisture at all.

She couldn't deny her companion was ruggedly handsome, with eyes the shade of Antwerp blue and chestnut brown hair that showed a bit of curl around the brim of his hat. An almost imperceptible bump on the bridge of his nose kept him from being too pretty, and she wondered if it was the result of a break during some kind of acrimonious scuffle or a rigorous game of rugby, or perhaps even American football. He looked the sporting, collegiate type. Muscular, self-assured – despite the dainty dogs – and yes, dangerously handsome.

No wonder she'd stepped right into his path, and yet she knew *(oh, she knew)* that this was the type of man to be avoided at all cost. Oliver had been broad with muscles and gloriously attractive too and look what that had gotten her.

The man cleared his throat a moment into the ride.

"Circumstances being what they are," he said formally. "Perhaps you'll allow me to introduce myself. I'm Chase Bostwick of Chicago. I'm staying at the Imperial Hotel, along with my mother and my sister. Please accept my apologies for that mishap in the street. Those are my mother's dogs," he added with a jut of square chin toward them, as if to apologize – again. His voice had a smooth timbre to it, rich and cultured, and she wondered if her sudden shiver was due to the chill of the air or the warmth of his tone.

Or the fact that she knew who he was, by name if not appearance. Egad, everyone in Chicago knew who the Bostwicks were. A.J. Bostwick, Sr., the family patriarch, was a self-made millionaire who, although not a Knickerbocker by birth, had married into high society and established his place among the Rockefellers and the Guggenheims. His sons – of which this was apparently one – had followed him into the family business and were earning their own reputations as men to be reckoned with. A sudden flush of embarrassment stole over her for she was certainly the first person in this man's life to shove him in the middle of a street, or to hurl slurs at his head.

An inauspicious beginning for her indeed.

"I accept your apology, Mr. Bostwick," she answered with a calmness she did not remotely feel, adding after a pause, "I'm sorry, as well. I should have been paying closer attention, but the rain impaired my vision." (*The rain and his damnable face.*)

"Yes, it's quite a deluge," he said. "And neither one of us with an umbrella it seems."

She wondered if he thought perhaps she should have one? A proper lady would've known – somehow –

that rain was imminent. Then again, so would a gentle-man, and he was definitely that, yet he had no umbrella either. She'd not mention it. She'd already insulted him once today. That seemed enough.

"Might I be so bold as to ask your name?" he asked after her hesitation. "As I mentioned, I would like to replace your art kit. I'll have it shipped to the hotel." He glanced at the splintered remnants in her lap, and she instinctively pulled them closer.

She paused again. It would mean nothing to him to purchase a new one. Lord knew he had the money, but that wasn't the point.

"I can't possibly accept a gift from you, Mr. Bost-wick. We're not properly acquainted. I don't know you." She only knew *of* him. And she also knew what *gifts* from men led to.

"It's not a gift. It's a replacement for something that has broken. If you won't accept it from me, I'll have my mother send it. Very proper."

He smiled at her, a charming, comfortable smile, and she knew, had this happened to her a year ago, she'd have responded in kind and trusted him implicitly because he had a sincere way about him. And dimples and tiny creases at the corners of his eyes. Everything about his easy, relaxed demeanor said, "I'm a decent person," and she'd never heard otherwise about any member of his family.

In fact, his father had made so sizable a donation to the Chicago Public Library after the great fire that A.J.'s portrait now hung in one of the reading rooms. She'd gazed at that painting so often it was a wonder she didn't recognize his son on sight, although truth be told, Jo had been more interested in the brushstrokes and artistic techniques, rather than the picture itself.

"It's not necessary, Mr. Bostwick. I appreciate your generosity, but I simply cannot accept."

Yes, a year ago she would have believed his sincerity and accepted his offer without hesitation, but now it was that very *appearance* of decency that made her wary. And a year ago, the art kit would not have meant as much to her.

Mr. Bostwick looked disappointed but nodded. "Of course. I understand. If you should change your mind, you need only send a note to Mrs. Constance Bostwick at the hotel, and she'll handle the rest."

"Thank you," she said, then turned her gaze to the window so he might not realize how badly she wanted to say yes.

They rode in silence for a few moments with nothing but the staccato rhythm of the rain tapping against the carriage roof in much the same rapid tempo as Jo's heart. She was nervous. Not because she thought herself in any personal danger, but a girl such as she, in her present dire circumstances, riding in a carriage with a man such as him, well, it made a person nervous.

One of the tiny dogs snuffled, repositioned, then settled back down with a woofy sigh. Jo continued to stare out the window, trying to regain her equilibrium while also trying to get a better look at the island that was to be her home for the next few months. She could see various buildings along the main thoroughfare. O'Doul's General Store. Callaghan's Leather Shop. Persimmon's Candy Emporium. She could see a military fort off in the distance, high on a hill as they passed a white-steepled church, a stable, and a hotel called The Island House that was so vast she could not imagine one more impressive. She'd been assured by her new employer, however, that the Imperial Hotel was the largest and most grand hotel on all of Wenniway Island, and that its guests expected only the finest in accommodations, food, and entertainment.

She was to be a part of that entertainment, hired to teach drawing and painting classes to eager debutantes and bored society matrons.

Well... sort of.

She had sort of been hired for that. There were a

few technicalities to work out but pressed between her corset and chemise was a signed contract offering the job to Emerson J. McKenna. And she was Emerson J. McKenna, so the job was legally hers. She'd tucked the contract there for safekeeping during her travels and hoped the ink hadn't run due to the rain. As if a smeared signature was the real problem. Uncertainty stirred in her veins, but she ignored it. Another method of coping.

"Is your name to remain a mystery then?" Mr. Bostwick asked pleasantly a moment later. "I find myself quite full of questions but if you'd rather not converse, I won't disturb you."

She tore her gaze from the scenery and looked back at him. It was no hardship, truly. In fact, she'd very much like to draw him, his face all interesting angles and planes, but talking to him was another matter entirely. Conversations in general, especially those full of questions, were not likely to go in her favor, but she could hardly refuse for fear of appearing rude, and perhaps she could even turn this to her advantage.

She smiled back, but not too brightly. It wouldn't do to appear too eager to make his acquaintance.

"Of course, you're not disturbing me, Mr. Bostwick. Please forgive me for being distracted by the landscape. I'm Emerson J. McKenna... *uh... Talbot*," she answered, suddenly not sure what to say after that. She was still getting used to the addition of Talbot. All things considered, it made her cringe to even say it, but that was, in fact, her name.

Like Mr. Bostwick, she was also *of Chicago* but not the parts he and *his people* traveled in. And, unlike him, she didn't actually *have people*. In fact, for most of her life it had been just her and her father in a cozy, modest house with lots of windows that let in abundant light and doors that were always open to visitors.

Until Oliver had come along.

Then for a while it had been the three of them. Until it wasn't.

Now it was just her. Because her father had died last year. A shock she was still growing accustomed to.

And Oliver?

Well, Oliver Talbot was her husband.

Sort of. There were some technicalities to work out there, too, and that was another shock she was still growing accustomed to. But, for her purposes on this island, she was married, so she squared her shoulders, extended a bold hand to Mr. Bostwick, and repeated herself, emphasizing the prefix.

"*Mrs.* Emerson Joan McKenna Talbot. I'm a portraitist and the new artist in residence at the Imperial Hotel."

If he was surprised by her position, he didn't show it, and if he was disappointed by her marital status, he didn't show that either and she reminded herself to be glad. That was the whole point, after all. To present herself to the Trillium Bay community as a seasoned artist and a devoted wife so they'd more readily accept her. No one would have allowed a single girl to travel alone all the way from Chicago to Trillium Bay, and they certainly wouldn't have hired a painter's *apprentice* to teach art classes at the Imperial Hotel, but she knew she was talented and an excellent teacher. She was entirely qualified, and being a married woman gave her gravitas. It gave her substance and morality and protection. Ironically, in this case, marriage gave her the freedom to do what she wanted to do.

And – legally – she was married. To Mr. Oliver Talbot.

It wasn't her fault he'd vanished in the wind just days after her father's funeral, leaving her with nothing to live on except the mercy of others and her own wits.

That part of her story she had no intention of sharing.

"It's a pleasure to officially meet you, Mrs. Talbot," Mr. Bostwick said smoothly. "And a portraitist, you say? How interesting. I confess I've no artistic talents whatsoever although my sister is modestly gifted. She's tried to educate me on the merits of the Impressionist movement but I'm a sorry student. So, is this your first summer on Trillium Bay, then? Or have you been here before?"

She bit back a smile because this was actually her first visit anywhere outside of Illinois, but she didn't want to admit that and sound provincial.

"Yes, this is my first trip to Trillium Bay although I've travelled quite a bit." That was vague enough to keep her out of trouble.

"Have you? What's your favorite destination?"

Drat. "Oh, I don't think I could choose just one place. Let's say… anywhere in Paris. What's your favorite destination?" Maybe she should let him do the talking.

"Truly my favorite? In all the world?" he asked, cocking his head as if to ponder.

"Yes."

"Fifty-five East Washington Street," he answered quickly, his eyes meeting hers and twinkling in a most disconcerting fashion. He was teasing her. He must be because fifty-five East Washington Street was surely a joke.

"Fifty-five East Washington… in Chicago?" Her voice flattened with skepticism.

He laughed, a nice rumbly sound. "Yes."

With all his wealth and connections, he must have been to a great many fabulous places, so this was indeed an odd choice, but perhaps Mr. Bostwick was an eccentric. That would explain the little dogs and his apparent penchant for walking in thunderstorms, yet she could not resist the question.

"Why?"

He shrugged, nonplussed by her apparent curiosity over his choice. "It's our company building. My office is on the top floor and the view is spectacular. I can see the lake for miles – when I remember to look up from my desk."

He was grinning now, and she found herself smiling back because it was impossible not to.

"And what do you do for work, Mr. Bostwick?" She already knew, of course. You couldn't live in Chicago and not know that Bostwick & Sons supplied investment capital to the likes of Vanderbilt, Stuyvesant, and Gould, but she wanted to see how he'd explain it. Surely, he'd boast like the industry mogul he was. With any luck, he'd talk the rest of the way to the hotel, and she wouldn't have to reveal another thing about herself while he'd reveal much, at least much about what kind of man he was.

It was an old artist's trick, a way to get the sitter relaxed during a portrait session and Jo was as good at drawing people *out* as she was at drawing them with charcoals. All she had to do was get them talking about whatever they loved the most. Apparently what Mr. Bostwick loved most was working.

"I work in finance," he said simply. "And where do you call home, Mrs. Talbot?"

His brief answer caught her off guard and she blurted out her response without thinking. "I'm from Chicago, too. Well, I used to live in Chicago, but I'll be moving to Paris in the autumn." *Or so she hoped.*

"Ah, another Chicagoan? I wonder if we might have crossed paths and never known."

"Perhaps," she said even while knowing they never had, and while also knowing he was just being polite for certainly he'd guessed they were not of the same circles. She *had* seen his mother at the milliner's once, though. Mrs. Constance Bostwick was purchasing the kind of garishly outlandish hat that only the very wealthy could claim as fashionable, a turquoise blue felt with black trim, lots of frilly ribbon, and an entire stuffed dove perched on the brim, as if the pitiful thing had simply landed there… and died.

The carriage lurched, and Jo tightened her grip on the art box, but not before a tube of paint slipped out and fell, plunking a dog on the head then hitting the floor. Mr. Bostwick picked it up easily and handed it to her and as he did so, she took note of the paint on her glove. She tried to wipe it away with her other hand but to no avail, and a sigh escaped before she could catch it. The brief buoyancy of her mood, lifted by their conversation, crashed down as she took in her ruined gown, the mud and paint stains beginning to dry and crack looking even worse, if possible, than they had when wet.

How? How was she to make herself presentable before meeting her new employer? How was she to stroll into the lobby of the Imperial Hotel looking as if she'd *rolled* there through the muck? She pressed her lips together tightly to still their trembling. Tears welled and threatened to spill but she was not the crying sort. Crying was for children and actresses, not grown women. Not *married* women. Not women with *jobs*.

Mr. Bostwick pulled a white silk handkerchief from inside his jacket pocket and offered it to her.

It was too fine. She shook her head. "No, I'm all right. Thank you."

He waved it at her ever so slightly. "You might want to dab just a bit, right here," he said tapping at his cheek with his other hand.

"Have I something on my face, too?" She gasped.

"Just a little paint. From your glove, I think. It's quite festive but not exactly the fashion at the Imperial."

It was thoughtful of him to treat the matter so lightly. He was trying to cheer her up with his teasing, it seemed, but she was suddenly despondent. Being plucky and optimistic took an immense amount of effort and she was tired from her travels.

"Oh," she sighed again, and let a tear escape although she quickly dashed it away. "It seems I am doomed to make a very poor first impression with my new employer." She reluctantly accepted the handkerchief and wiped at her cheek, but he shook his head and tapped his own cheek a little higher.

"Not quite," he said, reaching out. "Here. If you'll allow me."

She returned the handkerchief, and he opened the window of the carriage, extending his arm to let the silk dampen in the rain that still fell. Then he brought his hand back inside the carriage and leaned forward toward her.

"May I?" he asked.

She wanted to do it herself. It was beyond the boundaries of propriety for him to be so intimate with her, but he could see the mess she was, and she *(perhaps thankfully)* could not. She nodded her acquiescence like a sticky, reluctant child and found herself staring at his face as he, using just the cloth so that his fingers would not actually touch her, scrubbed gently at her cheek. He frowned after a moment and pressed a little harder.

"I'm sorry," he said as he rubbed. "It's a little stubborn."

"That's all right," she answered with another sigh. "So am I."

He smiled then, and his eyes met hers. If there was thunder or lightning or another lurch to the carriage, she wasn't certain, but something jolted her, and she moved away quickly.

ACKNOWLEDGMENTS

Even a short story requires a long list of people to thank, and my gratitude is boundless for those involved in this project. Thank you to Jordan Carson, Terri DeBoer, and the rest of the team at Wood TV 8 for letting me pester you with innumerable questions and loiter around your workplace. Who knew there was so much going on at four o'clock in the morning? Thank you to the storm chasers who post videos of their exploits which I watched on a repeating loop while drafting this story. Any errors in this novella with regard to meteorology or weather science are entirely my own.

Thank you to Jessica Poore, my editor-extraordinaire, who patiently fine-tuned this story. Thanks to Jamie Beck, Sonali Dev, Virginia Kantra, Sally Kilpatrick, Falguni Kothari, Priscilla Oliveras, Barbara Samuel O'Neal, and Liz Talley without whom this story would never have been completed. I cherish your advice and friendship.

Thank you, Jane Pierangeli, for early reads, late reads, coffee, conversation, and all the stuff.

And finally, thanks to my beautiful daughters, Webster Girl and Tenacious D. Your love and support bring me endless joy. Without you, none of the rest matters.

ALSO BY TRACY BROGAN

THE BOSTWICKS OF TRILLIUM BAY

ART OF THE CHASE

MAGIC OF MOONLIGHT

A DAISY IN BLOOM

THE TRILLIUM BAY SERIES

(CONTEMPORARY)

MY KIND OF YOU

MY KIND OF FOREVER

MY KIND OF PERFECT

THE BELL HARBOR SERIES

(CONTEMPORARY)

CRAZY LITTLE THING

THE BEST MEDICINE

LOVE ME SWEET

JINGLE BELL HARBOR (A novella)

STAND ALONE TITLES

HOLD ON MY HEART (Contemporary)

THE NEW NORMAL (Contemporary)

WEATHER OR KNOT (Contemporary novella)

HIGHLAND SURRENDER (Historical romance)

ABOUT THE AUTHOR

USA Today, Wall Street Journal, and Amazon Publishing bestselling author Tracy Brogan writes happily ever after stories full laughter and love. A three-time recipient of the Amazon Publishing Diamond award, a three-time finalist of the RWA® RITA award for excellence in romantic fiction, and a winner of the Booksellers Best award, Brogan's books, including both the Bell Harbor and Trillium Bay series, feature re-imagined versions of her favorite Michigan locations and have been translated into more than a dozen languages worldwide. Although best known for her laugh-out-loud contemporary romantic comedies, she's currently at work on several historical projects including a gilded age series – The Bostwicks of Trillium Bay, the long-awaited sequel to Highland Surrender, and a dual-timeline rom-com that just *may* include ghosts. (Psst… it totally has ghosts.)

Tracy Brogan Books. Witty. Whimsical. Wonderful.

Tracybrogan.com: Tracy Brogan

Email: tracybrogan1225@gmail.com